"Will you leave it alone?"

The sharpness in his voice made her jump.

"I'm simply—"

He whipped around. "I said drop it!"

Suddenly Zoe understood. There, in the confines of his pickup, she saw what he hid beneath the layers of unapproachability.

Pain.

Not physical pain, like his hip. No, this kind of pain ran deeper and stronger. It was the kind of pain medicine couldn't help. The kind that ripped a man's insides apart.

Zoe's own insides hurt for him. "I'm sorry," she replied, meaning for far more than her earlier intrusion.

She watched as he dragged a shaky hand across the back of his neck. Maybe it was her tone, or the fact that she'd apologized, but some of the edge left his voice. "I don't want to talk about it, okay?"

"Okay." She'd do what he wanted and let the subject drop. For now.

Dear Reader

You won't find the tiny island of Naushatucket on any map. When my heroine decides to escape the world, she does so to an imaginary representation based on several local islands. However, while her home base might be a product of her imagination, the breathtaking views she sees from her rooftop aren't. In my opinion, the Cape Cod and its islands have some of the most gorgeous ocean views in the world. Then again, being a lifelong Massachusetts resident, I might be a tad biased.

This book was a really hard book to write. Mainly because I felt it so very important to portray Jake Meyers' experiences with dignity and realism. Hopefully I did him justice.

The more I got to know Jake, the more I wanted to give him the happy ending he deserved. Enter Zoe Hamilton. She's not looking for love any more than Jake is. Who better to help a broken man heal than a woman who's dedicated herself to helping others? Of course Zoe's got her own baggage—baggage she hopes to escape with a summer at the shore. And, even though neither of them is looking for a relationship, they're about to find out fate thinks otherwise.

Finally, there's dear sweet Reynaldo. Zoe's beloved pet has trials of his own. I think reality was inspiring me. Turns out I have an even bigger soft spot for animals and sob stories than Zoe. I wrote this novel while nursing our own sick cat back from a brain infection.

I hope you enjoy Jake's and Zoe's story. Please drop me a line at Barbara@barbarawallace.com and let me know. I love hearing your feedback.

Regards

Barbara Wallace

Barbara Wallace has been a life-long romantic and daydreamer, so it's not surprising she decided to become a writer at age eight. However, it wasn't until a co-worker handed her a romance novel that she knew where her stories belonged. For years she limited her dream to nights, weekends, and commuter train trips, while working as a communications specialist, PR freelancer, and full-time mom. At the urging of her family she finally chucked the day job and pursued writing full time—and couldn't be happier.

Barbara lives in Massachusetts with her husband, their teenage son, and two very spoiled self-centred cats (as if there could be any other kind). Readers can visit her at www.barbarawallace.com and find her on Facebook. She'd love to hear from you.

To my editors—for being so patient while I worked to get this story just right

To the gals at the Medway Starbucks—for keeping me caffeinated at all hours of the day and night

And, as always, to my boys Pete and Andrew—you're my heroes.

CHAPTER ONE

JAKE MEYERS woke with a start, the smell of blood and sulfur still in his nostrils, his eyes searching the shadows for enemies who minutes before had been crystal clear. Kicking off his sweat-soaked covers, he focused on his heart slamming against his ribs. He willed his breathing to slow like they showed him in the hospital. Slow and easy. In. Out. Until the steady intake of air filling his lungs erased the sounds of screams.

Damn. After three and a half weeks without a nightmare, he'd thought they were behind him. No such luck.

With a ragged breath, he looked at the clock on his nightstand, ignoring the shudder triggered by the crimson glow. Five-fifteen. Well, at least this time it was close to dawn. His hip throbbed. The pain always flared more following a nightmare. If he were inclined to examine the reasons, he was sure he'd find some psychosomatic component, but in fact the reasons didn't really matter to him. Pain was pain. He grabbed the bottle of prescription painkillers off the nightstand and knocked over the photograph propped against the lamp as he did so. Reverently he put it back in place. The darkness obscured the image, but he didn't need light to see. He had the faces memorized. Every last one had been etched in his brain for eternity.

Hobbling into the kitchen, he saw a half pot of yesterday's coffee remained. Too tired and still too hazy from his dreams to make a fresh pot, he poured himself a cup and, as the liquid reheated in the microwave, stared out his back window. Outside, the island hung on the edge of morning, silent and gray, the world still except for the occasional screech of a gull diving toward the waves across the street.

And, of course, his thoughts. His thoughts were never silent.

The microwave beeped. Jake grabbed his coffee and stepped onto the back step, letting the overcast dampen his skin as he breathed in the silence. Dew dripped from the pine trees dotting his backyard, their green needles sparkling. A chipmunk poked its head out from beneath a root.

His purgatory shouldn't be so serene, he thought, not for the first time. As far as he was concerned, the world was wasting its early morning splendor on a dead man.

Give yourself time. That's what the doctors at the

VA hospital had told him. *Some wounds don't heal overnight.*

They were wrong, he thought, as he raised the cup to his lips. Some wounds don't heal at all.

"This hideaway of yours, does it have internet access?"

From behind her blue-rimmed glasses, Zoe Hamilton rolled her eyes. "Naushatucket's off the coast of Massachusetts, Caroline, not off the grid."

"If I can't read the label on a map, it might as well be." There was the muffled sound of a register on the other end of the phone. Caroline was out getting her midday latte. "Couldn't you hide out on one of the bigger islands, like Martha's Vineyard or Nantucket?"

"My family didn't own a rental property on Martha's Vineyard or Nantucket. Besides, isn't *remote* a hideout requirement?"

Judging from the extended sigh on the other end, her assistant disagreed. Zoe half listened to the noise while scanning the air around her. Caroline's check-in, though welcome, came at a bad time. "If you're worried about my column getting in on time, I have everything I need to work from here."

"I hope so. 'Ask Zoe's' readers will be distraught if they don't get regular posts from their favorite answer lady."

Answer fraud, more like. "Don't worry. They'll get their responses." Poor trusting saps.

A flash of black caught the corner of her eye; she spun around, eyes following the trajectory.

Success. Her target had landed. The rest of the phone call would have to wait. "I hate to hang up on you, Caroline, but unless there's anything else, I was in the middle of something when you called."

"Fine," Caroline replied with another dramatic sigh. "I know a brush-off when I hear one. Just promise me you won't spend all your time on that island crying your eyes out. That bastard isn't worth the effort."

"I won't." On that point, they both agreed. Thinking of Paul churned up a lot of responses these days, but tears weren't one of them. At least, not anymore.

After making a few additional promises, including assuring Caroline she wouldn't become a complete hermit, Zoe said goodbye and clicked off the phone. "Okay, Birdy, now it's your turn."

From its perch above the open sliding glass door, a swallow, her nemesis for the past half hour, stared back unflinchingly. The creature had been circling the room through her entire phone call, steadfastly ignoring the escape route Zoe had provided. Finally, the bird stopped to rest, giving Zoe her chance.

"I really don't know why you're being so stubborn."

She slipped off the silk scarf she'd been using to hold back her thick dark hair. Immediately a shock of bangs flapped over her glasses. She blew them out of her field of vision and took a step closer, careful not to move too quickly.

"The door is open. All you have to do is fly out and you'll be free."

Her plan was to wave the scarf, using the color and motion to steer the bird off the molding and out the patio door. The swallow, however, had a different plan and, as soon as Zoe lunged forward, decided to dart straight for her. Letting out a screech, Zoe ducked. The bird flew overhead, careening off a ceiling beam before knocking into the mantel and flying up the chimney.

Zoe rolled her eyes. "You've got to be kidding."

When she had first decided to hide out for the summer, buying her parents' Naushatucket property sounded exciting, romantic even. What better place to heal a broken heart than an isolated cottage by the sea? Visions of long reflective walks along the shore and cozy nights by campfires came to mind. Instead, she discovered that her mother had let the property deteriorate since remarrying. Her childhood vacation paradise had become a sorely neglected Cape house with dusty furniture and sand-crusted windows. Screenless windows, she might add, a fact she had discovered when she tried to clear the house of stale air. Enter Birdy, who apparently had been lying in wait for someone to open one of them.

Pushing her glasses back on the bridge of her nose, she knelt down on the hearth and readied herself for round two.

"It's not that I don't appreciate the company and all," she called up, "but Reynaldo and I weren't planning on sharing the house with a bird, and I'm guessing you're not keen on sharing with us. So what do you say you fly out the nice wide door I opened for you?"

Her answer was a panicked flutter of wings against brick.

"Fine. Don't listen to reason." Moving on to Plan B—or C as the case might be—she grabbed the poker from the fireplace set. A loud noise ought to do the trick. Reaching up into the flue, she rattled the poker back and forth. The commotion set off more fluttering, followed by a rustling sound. Zoe looked up.

A shower of creosote, dust and feathers rained down.

Soot covered her from head to toe, clinging to her sweaty skin like iron filings on a magnet. Dust filled her nose. Her mouth tasted like the inside of an ashtray. Coughing, she backed away into the fresh air. Meanwhile, the swallow continued flapping inside the chimney.

Great. This was what she got for trying to help. Hot, sweaty and soot-on. You'd think she'd learn.

"This isn't over, Birdy," she muttered. She reached for the abandoned scarf to clean off her glasses.

"Excuse me."

Zoe jumped. Either Birdy had some serious testosterone issues or she had a guest. A blur in the doorway told her the latter. Slipping her glasses back on, she saw a man standing in the doorway. Tall and lean, with ruddy, weathered skin, he wore the standard island old-timer uniform—faded jeans and an equally faded long-sleeve T-shirt.

He lifted a guilty-looking dachshund to eye level.

Zoe recognized the dog immediately. "Reynaldo! You're supposed to be sleeping in the kitchen."

"I found him digging around my backyard." From the look on his face, he wasn't happy about it, either.

"Sorry about that. He normally isn't a wanderer. Must be the new location." She moved to retrieve the squirming pooch from the stranger's grip before something else happened. "I'm Zoe Brodsk—I mean, Hamilton." She had to stop using her married name. "I just bought the place. I'd shake your hand, but as you can see…"

No need finishing the explanation; the soot spoke for itself. He didn't look like he wanted to shake her hand anyway.

Now that she had a closer view, she realized her neighbor was younger than her initial impression implied. Hair she'd mistaken for silver was really sun-bleached blond. And what she thought was aged ruddiness was really a series of pale scars, several small ones running across the bridge of his nose and one along the curve of his cheekbone. The most prominent was a deep mark that cut from his left temple to the center of his left brow, stopping just above a pair of hard, emerald eyes. Eyes whose intense gaze currently had her rooted to the spot.

Reynaldo squirmed in her arms, sniffing and trying to lick at her ash-covered cheeks. Since adding dog drool to her already filthy face wasn't on her to-do list, Zoe set him down. In a flash, the dachshund ran to the fireplace and began barking. His dancing around reminded her how she'd gotten soot-covered to begin with.

Turning back to her neighbor, she asked, "You don't know anything about capturing birds, do you?"

"Why, you got one of those that escaped while you weren't watching, too?"

"No." For the sake of neighborliness, she decided to ignore the comment. "I've got one stuck in my fireplace that needs rescuing."

He shoved his hands into his jeans pockets, a posture that accentuated a pair of long muscular arms. "How do you know?"

"That I have a bird in the chimney? I saw it fly up there." No need to add that she was the reason why.

"No, I mean how do you know it needs rescuing?"

"Because he's *stuck*. I can hear his wings flapping against the brick."

"Doesn't mean he wants your help."

Was this guy serious? "How else is he going to get free?"

"How about on his own?"

"You're assuming he's capable of freeing himself."

"You're assuming he isn't."

Zoe brushed at her bangs, more to prevent herself rolling her eyes than anything. Who cared what she was assuming? The poor bird needed her help. She wasn't getting into some pointless argument with a man who couldn't be bothered to introduce himself.

"Either way, I need to help this bird out," she said, dismissing the man. Hey, she was from the city; she could be as abrupt and unsocial as the next person. "Thank you for bringing Reynaldo home. I'll make sure he stays out of your backyard."

"Good."

Good. Not *thank you,* but *good.* Somebody needed to work on his people skills. Her "neighbor's" dearth of social graces, however, would have to wait. She had more important tasks to focus on. Assuming their conversation had ended, she returned her attention to the fireplace.

"Leave the room."

"Excuse me?" She frowned at the man from over her shoulder.

"Noise will keep the bird riled up," he replied. "Especially the barking. The two of you should leave. Once the room settles down, the bird will come out."

"What if it doesn't?" From the way the bird was flapping, it might beat itself to death before calming down. "What then?"

"Then I guess you'll find out the first time you light a fire."

Zoe's mouth dropped open. She whirled around to protest, but the stranger had already slipped out the door. So much for the friendly neighborhood welcome wagon. First time you light a fire, indeed.

"No way I'm waiting until the thing burns up in a fire to know if he escaped," she told Reynaldo. "He needs our help now."

With that, she grabbed the poker and readied for another round. "Time to come out, Birdy!" She clanged the poker around the chimney a second time. Then a third.

A loud rustling sound replied, followed by several high-pitched whistles. There was a rush of noise and the swallow came bombing out.

"Ha!" Triumphant, she wiped away the fresh

batch of soot with the back of her hand. The bird *had* needed her help. She watched as it circled the room once, then twice, before heading for the open patio door.

Where it promptly landed on the door-frame molding. In the exact place this rescue mission had begun.

Jake stomped across the yard, up his steps and straight to his refrigerator for a cold beer. Who cared if it was before noon? The day was already shaping up to be a damn lousy one, and that was before he found the dachshund digging around his yard.

He'd come to Naushatucket for solitude. Which was why living next to a rental property suited him just fine. Temporary vacationers seldom offered more than a wave and a nod, too busy cramming their visits with summer fun to attempt conversation. He didn't need a neighbor moving in with her pet and her cheery smile. Hopefully, she'd only stay the summer.

The letter he'd been reading was on the counter where he'd dropped it, the opening paragraph still visible.

Dear Captain Meyers,
As you may have read in the local paper, the Flag Day Committee is honoring our area heroes....

He crumpled the paper in his fist. Heroes, huh? Then they didn't need him.

Dear Zoe,
I'm in love with a man I work with. He's wonderful. Handsome, funny, smart. Problem is, no matter what I do, I can't get him to see me as anything more than the woman in the next office. I know if I can just get his attention, he'll see what a terrific match we would make. He's not dating anyone. In fact, I've overheard him complaining he can't find the right woman. What can I do to make him see the right woman is me?
Invisible

Dear Invisible,
What can I say? Guys are blind idiots. They can't see a good woman even if she's under their noses. And when they do meet the right girl, they'll treat her like dirt and dump her for the first blonde with big breasts that crosses the fairway. Might as well learn this now and save yourself the heartache. If you want love, get a pet.
Zoe

Zoe stared at the answer she just typed. Probably not the answer Invisible wanted to hear. After all, she was

Zoe of 'Ask Zoe,' the woman with all the answers on love and life. If only they knew. What was that old saying? Those who can't, write advice columns? She pressed Delete, erasing her bitter words from the screen if not from her heart.

Normally she didn't have a problem coming up with the kind of advice her readers wanted to hear, but tonight the answers wouldn't come.

Who was she kidding? The answers hadn't come for weeks. Not since Paul made a mockery out of every answer she ever gave.

Reynaldo barked. Zoe gave a smile and scooped him onto the sofa. "Good old Reynaldo. You'll always want me, right? We'll muddle through, you, me and the occasional stray bird."

It had taken thirty minutes, but the swallow finally flew the coop, disappearing while she was busy relocating Reynaldo to an upstairs bedroom. She swore the creature timed its exit specifically to spite her.

Now clean and tired, she lay wrapped in a fleece throw trying to keep the evening chill at bay. She'd forgotten how chilly island nights could be during the late spring. Come next month, heat and humidity would make the sea breeze a welcome visitor, but tonight the chill clung to the last of the crisp air with typical New England stubbornness. There was a fireplace, but her neighbor's comment had left her reluctant to build one. Bad enough she'd imagined his "told you so" when the bird flew away. She didn't need to prove him right with a chimney fire, too. Until she had the chimney cleaned, the fleece and Reynaldo would have to do. She pulled the blanket a little higher.

Meanwhile her secondary heating source was having trouble settling down, insisting instead on walking up and down the length of her body like a stubby-legged cat. The restlessness meant one of two things—either food or a bathroom break—and since he'd emptied his food dish twenty minutes ago…

She groaned. "All right, let's go."

Outside, the night was gray but for the porch light next door. Zoe stood under her own burnt-out light and watched the moths flitting toward the beam. Despite being the only source of light, there was a somberness to her neighbor's house. Maybe it was the lack of color on its gray, weathered shingles or the memory of its owner's unsmiling face. The memory of bright emerald eyes came floating back.

At the bottom of the steps, Reynaldo sniffed the grass uninterestedly before trotting to the fence dividing the properties.

"That's far enough," she said, calling the dachshund back. After three years together, she liked to believe her little rescue dog would respond to her voice. Wishful thinking, but she liked deluding herself. Why not? She excelled at it, didn't she?

"We said we'd stay in our own yard, remember? How about we try and keep our promise?"

Suddenly the sound of a back door opening breached the quiet. Zoe's insides stilled. Through a gap in the posts, she spied a crop of sun-bleached hair and a somber profile. Funny, only a moment before she'd been thinking his yard dark. Illuminated by the white cone of his porch light, he looked brighter than bright in the gray. Zoe swore she could see the flash of his green eyes as he stared out into the night. In his hand, he held an amber bottle.

Curious, Zoe watched as he drank his beer and studied whatever it was he saw in his backyard. Or was he searching? Though really too far away for her to truly see, he seemed to be focused on a point far past his property line.

After a minute, he raised the bottle one last time and turned back inside. With the flick of a switch, the light disappeared, leaving Zoe and Reynaldo alone in the darkness.

She definitely had to clean the chimney. Waking up to a foggy, gray morning, it took Zoe less than a second to make the decision. Granted, she'd probably only need the fireplace for a week or so, until the summer heat arrived, but that was one week too long to do without. Shivering under the covers in flannel pj's and a sweatshirt was not how she wanted to spend her nights. Especially since Reynaldo insisted on making a predawn bathroom trip every morning.

"I swear, you have a bladder the size of a pea," she said to him.

Palming her coffee mug, she returned to her list. Charles and her mother weren't kidding when they said they'd ignored the property the past couple years. Since Rey had her awake, she decided to make a list of home repairs she needed to tackle. Clearly, Rey needed a dog run, if for no other reason than to keep him out of their green-eyed neighbor's yard. The memory of his laser-sharp gaze sent a tremor down her spine, where it pooled in uncomfortable warmth at the base.

Definitely, a dog run. And a new light for the back door so she wouldn't have to stand in the dark while Rey relieved himself. Those repairs she could do herself. But the chimney... Sadly, chimney sweeping was out of her purview.

"Guess that means I need to find a handyman, Rey. Think this island has one?" Pitcher's Hole was more a fishing hole than a town, though she had noticed a small hardware store near where the ferry docked. "I imagine that's as good a place as any to start asking around. If nothing else, maybe we can find a portable heater for the bedroom." If the dated electrical system could handle the extra voltage.

Getting dressed had never been a big production for her. Less so now that she had no one to impress. A quick brush of her hair, a splash of water on her face and she was done. As she adjusted her glasses, she stared at the reflection in the mirror. Unimpressive blue eyes and hair badly needing a trim stared back. No wonder Paul had only wanted her money. Maybe if she'd spent a little more time, worn a little lipstick…

Zoe shook the thought from her head. She could play what-if 'til the cows came home—Paul would still be out of her life.

Besides, this summer was supposed to be about healing, not bemoaning her new—and no doubt permanent—single status. Better to focus on tasks at hand.

The kitchen was conspicuously empty when she came downstairs. "Rey?"

Barking sounded from outside. Looking to the screen door, she saw the latch had failed to catch. Another item for the to-do list, along with the dog run.

"The size of a pea," she said, stepping outside. "I swear, Rey, the size of a pea."

Reynaldo didn't respond. In fact, much to her dismay, he was nowhere in sight.

Oh, please let him be sniffing around the side bushes and not exploring next door. It was way too early in the morning to face those laser beam eyes.

"You again!"

Zoe groaned. No such luck.

* * *

There wasn't a trace of a smile on her neighbor's face as he held up a very contrite Reynaldo.

Zoe was pretty sure her own face mirrored the dog's. "Sorry. He snuck out while I was in the other room."

"Seems to happen a lot."

Twice. It had happened twice. "He doesn't usually wander far from home. For some reason he has an affinity to your backyard." She forced a smile. "Must be something over there he finds appealing."

Though for the life of her, she didn't know what.

Without so much as cracking a glimmer of a smile, her neighbor—whose name she still didn't know— thrust Reynaldo in her direction. "There's an invention called a leash. I suggest you buy one."

I suggest you buy one. Zoe fought the urge to smirk. At least one of them should try to act civilly. "I'm installing a dog run today."

If he appreciated the gesture, it didn't show on his face. He simply grunted what sounded like an acknowledgment before turning away.

Distracted by the bird and other things yesterday, she'd missed it, but her neighbor had a limp. He clearly favored his right leg. Between this and the scars... Whatever had happened to him, was it the reason for the prickliness? she wondered. Because so far the man had been a six-foot roll of barbed wire, sharp and impossible to approach. With any luck, once she installed the dog run and had Reynaldo back in check, she wouldn't have to cross his thorny path again.

CHAPTER TWO

NAUSHATUCKET ISLAND wasn't a major Cape Cod island. That title belonged to its larger sisters, Nantucket and Martha's Vineyard. Only a handful of its population lived there year-round. Most were like Zoe: transient residents who wanted a summer at the islands but without the big island crowds. As a little girl, Zoe had spent a summer here with her parents when her father was in remission. Back then Pitcher's Hole consisted of a fish market, an ice-cream shop and the ferry station. It didn't consist of much more now, though there were a few additional stores, including the hardware store she had seen yesterday. She headed there first, hoping the staff might know of someone on the island who did repair work. If not, she'd have to bring in someone from New Bedford or one of the other big islands, a cost she wasn't keen on absorbing.

Turned out Pitcher's Hole Hardware was more a marine supply shop than an actual hardware store. Brass fittings and anchor line seemed to be the order of the day. It was also, to Zoe's chagrin, smaller than small, with rows so narrow only one person at a time could navigate them.

Of course, the claustrophobic space might have been tolerable had her neighbor not limped in shortly after her. By merely walking in, the man absorbed all the surrounding air, as if his six-foot frame were twice that size. Zoe, who'd been perusing the rope section, ducked deeper into the aisle. She didn't know why, but his appearance unnerved her. She blamed the barbed-wire layers, layers she could feel from her hiding place as he approached the front counter.

"Morning, Jake," the manager greeted. *So that was his name. Jake.* She'd pictured something far more intimidating. *Jake* was a dependable, solid name, a name you could count on.

In a way, she was surprised the manager and he were on a first-name basis. There was such a solitary air about him, she could easily imagine him never speaking to anyone.

"You called about the clamp connector?"

Case in point, thought Zoe.

The manager took his abruptness in stride. "Your order came over on the boat yesterday. Let me get it."

He disappeared into the back room, leaving Jake alone at the counter. Leaving the two of them alone in the store. Why she found this fact unsettling Zoe didn't know, but she was determined to ignore both

the man and her reaction to his proximity. She returned her gaze to the rope display, attempting to
calculate the length she would need for Rey's run,
but trapped in the cramped space of the store, her
neighbor's presence pulled her attention back. Try
as she might she found herself stealing glances in
his direction. He had, she realized, the most perfect
posture she'd ever seen. No wonder he loomed large.
Shoulders straight, head high—he commanded attention even in a faded flannel shirt and jeans. She
supposed that explained her fascination. Curmudgeon
though he might be, he was a compelling one.

The manager returned carrying a pair of packages
containing items Zoe couldn't identify. "Here you
go. Already on your account so you're all set. By the
way, did Kent Mifflin contact you about the Flag Day
dedication?"

"Yeah, he did."

"Great, so…"

"Thanks for the clamp connectors."

Zoe watched as Jake gathered his packages and
limped out the door. If he noticed the store manager's
disappointed expression, his actions didn't show it.

"You looking for something special, miss?"

The question caused her to start. So engrossed
had she been in observing her neighbor walk across
the street, she'd missed the manager coming to join
her. Recovering, she pointed to the rope. "I need ten
feet," she said, "and a couple of swivel clips."

"Sure thing." Grabbing a pair of cutters, he began measuring out the length. "You moored at the dock?"

"Setting up a dog run." *So I don't annoy the man who just left here.* "I'm spending the summer on the island."

"You picked a great place. Naushatucket's a great place to unwind."

"I know. My parents used to come summers a long time ago. I just bought their place."

Bringing her to the other reason for her hardware store visit. "Place is a little run-down, though. I'm hoping to make some repairs while I'm here. You wouldn't be able to recommend a handyman, would you?"

"Sure can," the manager replied, coiling the rope between his hand and his elbow. "Best on the island. You can tell him Ira sent you. That way he'll know you're a resident."

"Terrific. Do you know if he sweeps chimneys?"

"Oh, I'm sure he does. He handles just about everything else."

The mere thought of using her fireplace warmed Zoe's inside. With any luck she could get her chimney swept and be basking in warmth in a few days.

"Too bad I didn't talk to you sooner," Ira continued. "I could have introduced you before he left."

"Left?" The warmth inside her began to fade,

replaced by a prickling sensation on the back of her neck. She had a bad feeling Ira was about to say something she didn't want to hear.

"Yeah, he was just here. Name's Jake Meyers." He handed her the coiled length of rope. "You won't find a better contractor on the islands."

Zoe forced a smile. Her neighbor was the handyman.

Oh, yay.

It was a simple business transaction. He had a service; she needed that service. Nothing to get worked up about.

So why was she?

Crossing the line from her front yard to Jake's, Zoe had to forcibly calm herself down. Which was absurd, really. So what if their last two encounters had involved more glaring than conversation? The man was a contractor, and she was a potential customer. She had every right to knock on his front door. There was absolutely no reason for her pulse to be beating so quickly.

In the daylight, the house was far less intimidating. Trimmed green grass and flowering shrubs made the gray seem less bleak, as did the farmer's porch. The building still wasn't bright and cheery by any stretch of the imagination, but the potential was there lurking beneath the surface. More important, the house was well maintained, which boded well for Mr. Meyers's

skills. All she needed to do was swallow her unchar-
acteristic bout of nerves and hire him.

The door swung open before her fist could greet
the wood. "If you're looking for your dog, he's not
here."

His glare burned straight through her and singed
her resolve. Was it too late to back away?

"Reynaldo's locked in the house," she managed
to squeak out. Using her glasses as a stall tactic, she
repositioned the frames while she searched for her
voice. "I figured he was better off staying out of your
way."

"You figured right."

He propped himself against the door frame. For
some reason, Zoe's eyes went to the hands pressed
against the molding. As a means of assessing his
skill, she told herself. His long fingers curved around
the lip of the molding, elegant despite the windburn
and scarring. They looked like very capable hands.

Strong hands.

Quickly she looked back to his face only to find
herself trapped by his hard stare. "Still trying to 'save'
your bird? Or is today a new rescue mission?"

"Neither." Zoe could already feel herself chafing
under his scrutiny. It was as if he were trying to push
her out of his yard with his eyes. "My chimney needs
sweeping."

"That so?"

"At least I think so. The house has been kind of neglected the past couple years...."

"I hadn't noticed."

She flashed a smirk. "Anyway, since the nights are still a little cool, I'd like to use the fireplace and I thought it wise to have the chimney cleaned out before I do. I was at the hardware store this morning—"

"I know."

Meaning he'd noticed her. Had he seen her staring, too? Her stomach did a weird kind of somersault. Swift and sudden, the reaction left her flustered. Once again, she hid behind adjusting her glasses. "Anyway, I asked at the store about a handyman and the manager suggested you. Said you were the best on the island. I was hoping I could hire you."

Jake drew his lips into a tight line. "Hmm."

Not exactly the most enthusiastic response in the world. Either he didn't need the business or—she hated the pebble of insecurity that accompanied her next thought—he didn't want hers. "Are you available? If it's a problem, I'll make sure Reynaldo stays out of your way."

"Because you've done such a bang-up job of that so far."

"He's a little worked up because it's a new location. I assure you, I'm capable of keeping my dachshund under control." The last comment came out sharper than necessary, but she couldn't help it. She didn't appreciate his tone. In fact, now that she thought about it, she didn't appreciate his entire attitude.

"On second thought, never mind." Screw his skills and sexy, capable-looking hands. She didn't need the hassle. "I'll ask the manager to recommend someone else."

"He won't."

"That so?" she replied, quoting him.

"There's a reason Ira said I was the best contractor on the island."

"Really? And what's that?"

"I'm also the only one."

In a flash, Zoe's bravado disappeared. "The only one?"

Jake shrugged. "You might find one or two more in a couple weeks, when the summer population shows up, if you can get one of them to take a break from their vacation."

"In a couple weeks I won't need fires to warm the house."

"No, you probably won't."

Zoe sighed. She was stuck with Mr. Attitude whether she liked it or not. That is, if he took the job. She might have snapped away her opportunity. She offered her best contrite smile. "I don't suppose I can get a do-over?"

"I don't believe in do-overs."

"Oh." So much for that.

"But I will sweep your chimney. Gonna have to go to the Vineyard for supplies, though."

"Oh, that's fine." Relief made her far more agreeable than she should be. "Buy whatever you need."

"I take cash or check. No credit."

"No problem. Give me a working fireplace and I'll pay you in solid gold bars if that's what you want." In the back of her mind she knew she should be getting more information before agreeing to his terms. Like how much he charged, for example. But the promise of a warm bed trumped good business. Besides, if he were the only handyman on the island, which was entirely possible, given the lack of full-time population, then she didn't have a whole lot of negotiation room anyway. "Anything to avoid shivering through the night."

His eyes swept the length of her and Zoe found herself wondering just how she would define the term *anything*. It had been a long time since a man looked at her like she was a woman. At least not without a hidden agenda.

"Cash or check will suffice."

So much for being looked at like a woman. "Right." The deflated sensation in the pit of her stomach was *not* disappointment. Not that kind anyway.

Unsure what to do next, especially with the embarrassment creeping along her skin, she toed the welcome mat and brushed the bangs off her frames. "Well then," she said, clearing her throat. "I'll set up things when you're done." A graceful exit, this was not.

Worse, he continued to stare at her. Hot and hard. Like he was trying to read under her skin. It made her insides all jumpy.

"I'll..." Her voice caught *again*. "I'll let you get back to what you were doing..."

"Where are you going?"

The question came abruptly, sounding more like a command, and froze her just as she was about to step off the porch. "Um, home?" she offered.

"Not if you want your chimney cleaned. Told you, we have to go to the Vineyard for supplies."

"We?" How on earth did she factor in?

"I don't carry a line of credit at the Vineyard store."

"So?" She still wasn't sure what that had to do with her going to the Vineyard or anywhere else with him.

"So," he said, pushing away from the door, "someone's got to pay for your supplies."

Which was why, a half hour later, Zoe found herself ducking the spray as they cruised across the sound in Jake's powerboat. On a good day, the ride took forty-five minutes. It might as well have lasted for eternity since her companion was a stone-faced statue. For the first few minutes, she tried to engage him in conversation, but after the third consecutive one-word answer, she gave up, settling instead for stealing glances at his silent profile.

She had to admit the man knew how to handle a boat. Yet again, she found her attention drawn to his hands and to the way the wheel glided effortlessly under his fingers. He was less steering the boat than commanding it to do his bidding.

Commanding. At the hardware store, she'd thought of him compelling. Now she had a second word to describe him.

There was something else about him, too. A quality she couldn't name. Originally, she'd have said *prickly,* but studying him now, the word didn't quite fit. Oh, he was prickly—okay, he was unfriendly—but her gut told her something about the prickliness didn't ring true. Why she thought that she couldn't say, but her gut said there was more to Jake Meyers than met the eye.

And we all know how well your gut works, right, Zoe? She cringed, remembering how certain she'd been about Paul. The way she'd defended him to everybody. *You don't know him like I do. He needs me.* Paul had needed her all right. Needed her money.

Across the water, Zoe spied the shores of Martha's Vineyard closing in. Come three weeks from now, part-time residents and vacationers would jam both the waterways and the tiny island's streets. At the moment, however, the island belonged to the year-round residents, leaving the bay quiet and half-full.

Jake steered his boat around West Chop and toward Vineyard Haven. About ten yards out, he slowed the engine, engulfing the day in even greater silence as they glided toward an empty slip.

Finally, a chance to do something besides sit with her thoughts. Scrambling forward, she grabbed the rope, and soon as they were close enough, stepped onto the dock. It'd been a while since she'd done any kind of boating, but the lessons came back quickly enough as she deftly tied them off. She then moved starboard, and repeated the task. When finished, she looked up to see Jake studying her handiwork. The glasses obscured part of his expression but she could see he was surprised. The knowledge caused a bubble of pride in her chest. She waited while Jake secured the rest of the boat, thinking, as he moved around, that for a man with a bad leg he carried himself with a great deal of grace. Then again, was she really surprised?

"Store's about a mile up, on Main Street," he said, when he joined her on the pier.

Zoe looked across the parking lot to the tree-lined street. A handful of cars drove by, turning right and disappearing. "I take it we're walking," she said, glad she had thought to wear comfortable shoes today.

"Unless you've got a better idea."

Unfortunately, she didn't.

Jake had already taken off through the parking lot and she had to scramble to catch up. A difficult task, given he had a foot of height on her and she had to take two steps to match one of his.

"Hey!" she called out. "How about we slow it down a bit?" If she had to walk, fine, but she wasn't going to sprint the entire way.

He stopped and if she were a betting woman, she'd say the sag in his shoulders was caused by frustration. There went any points she might have scored back at the dock. "Some of us have shorter legs," she pointed out, in case he'd missed the obvious.

They fell back into step, albeit at a slightly slower pace. Zoe entertained herself by studying the clapboard houses and brick sidewalk. About a hundred yards in, she lost interest and decided to give conversation another shot. "I've never been to this section of the Vineyard. Do you make the trip often?"

"Often enough."

"Downside of island living, I suppose. I should have thought about that before moving to one." She'd only been thinking of getting away. "On the other hand, now I know why my mother didn't make repairs. Too much trouble getting building supplies."

"Most people manage."

"Most people aren't sequestered in an Atlanta townhome. My mother hasn't come north since she remarried. The house was always more my father's anyway. He was the one who planned on using it every summer. At least he did, before he got sick. I forgot about the place myself until my divorce. Then I bought the place from her and—"

Dear God, she was babbling. Worse than babbling, she was oversharing. "Have you lived on the island long?"

"Long enough."

Not surprisingly, Jake did the opposite and *under*shared. She plowed on, not willing to return to silence. "Growing up, my dad called Naushatucket an undiscovered paradise. Of course, I only cared about the beach, but now I can see what he meant. A person can really escape from it all there, can't he?"

"Used to, anyway."

A pointed hint. They stepped off the curb and out of the corner of her eye, she saw Jake grimace. "Leg bothering you?" The question came out before she could stop herself.

"No."

A lie if ever she heard one. It was obvious from the way his mouth pulled in a tight line every time he stepped off his right foot. She stared at him, silently calling him on it, until he could no longer ignore her.

"Hip," he said. "And it always bothers me."

"I'm sorry."

"Why? It's not your hip."

No, but he was in obvious pain, and that made her feel bad. "Look, you don't need to do the chimney today if..."

Wrong thing to say. Sunglasses or no sunglasses, she could feel the heat of his stare bearing down on her. "You asked me to clean your chimney today—I'll clean the damn thing today."

With that, he picked up his pace as if proving a point. "I'll live with the pain."

Jake's hip throbbed so much he had to clench his jaw from the pain. A doctor would probably tell him he was being a stubborn fool. That he was making himself suffer needlessly. Of course, Jake would debate that last word. *Needlessly.* He was pretty damn certain his suffering was justified. Though he did feel a little bad for dragging the Bird Whisperer along.

Speaking of which... He felt her cast another look in his direction, setting his nerves on edge. Since his discharge he'd gotten all kinds of looks. The discreet. The openly gaping. The disgustingly compassionate. All of them with some sort of awe, as if he were a freaking hero.

Little Miss Bird-Whisperer's looks, though... God, but he could feel her pale blue eyes scanning his profile. His skin prickled with the awareness. Without turning, he could picture them wide and curious. Like she was trying to see inside him or something. It irritated the hell out of him. What had made him say yes to her job offer in the first place?

He had bills to pay, that was what. And hanging around the house did nothing but make his thoughts loud, and they were loud enough this morning as it was. A project was exactly what he needed to drown them out for a little while.

The morning overcast had finally burned off, allowing the sun to take hold and warm the air. Jake felt the sweat starting to trickle down the back of his neck. Zoe had peeled off her grey sweatshirt. Jake tried not to notice her bright orange T-shirt or how it fit a little too snugly over her breasts. He was trying not to pay attention to her at all—a desire she seemed intent on disrupting at every opportunity.

"How much farther 'til we get to the store?" she asked.

"Couple blocks." Normally the walk didn't take that long; this morning it was taking forever. He blamed his impossible-to-ignore companion.

"Mind if we stop at that coffee shop on the corner first? I don't know about you, but I could use a cold drink. I'll even pa—"

The words were barely out of her mouth when she stumbled over a dip in the sidewalk. Jake reacted automatically, reaching out with a hand to grab her arm, and caught her as she fell forward. It was a mistake. Catching her meant looking in her direction. Suddenly he had an up-close view of what he'd been trying to ignore. He saw freckles kissing the bridge of a windblown nose and strands of black hair wisping over surprised eyes. A long-dormant awareness, unbidden and unwanted, began stirring somewhere deep inside him.

Quickly, he let go. "You can get your drink if you want. I'll meet you at the hardware store," he said, shoving his hands in his jeans pockets.

To hell with his no-credit policy. Next time he'd make this trip alone and bill her.

Unlike the store in Pitcher's Hole, this particular store was large and well-stocked. Jake used the place whenever he had a large or unusual job. He liked it because they left him alone and he could therefore avoid small talk, something his companion apparently thrived on. As soon as they walked in the door, she'd sought out a clerk and was currently engrossed in a conversation about outdoor lighting. At least it was supposed to be about lighting. He hadn't thought that a terribly amusing topic, and they seemed to be chuckling a little too heartily. Somewhere in between laughs, he caught the word *dachshund*.

"I was telling Javier how Reynaldo seems determined to hang out in your yard," Zoe said when he approached. "He thinks Rey's chasing chipmunks."

"My cousin had a dachshund," the clerk said. "They're big hunters."

"What's wrong with the chipmunks in his yard?" Jake grumbled.

The young man shrugged. "Where's the fun in that?"

Not in his yard, that's where. "Got what I need," he said to Zoe.

The look she gave the clerk was apologetic, as if *he* were the one holding up the process. "Thanks for the suggestion," she said, smiling. "But I'll go with the single spotlight. Javier recommended I get a double one to better keep an eye on Reynaldo, but that might shine a little too brightly into your backyard."

She turned her smile on him, and Jake could practically see the sarcasm behind her expression.

Suddenly they were interrupted by a pair of men in maintenance uniforms. Jake was about to tell them to find another clerk when he realized they weren't there for hardware supplies. Their faces were pale and somber. *"É Ernesto,"* they said. *"Está morto."*

Morto. Dead. His body began to shake. There were more words. *Accident. Car.* Bits and pieces of an explanation that drifted to him from far away, like words whispered in a tunnel. Black closed in him, eating away reality.

Get out. Take cover.

No, no, that wasn't right. *Get to fresh air.* He needed fresh air.

Miles away he saw a doorway. And light. Light meant safety. *There. Go there.* His thoughts were thick and muddled as he staggered toward it, faintly aware of a bell ringing as he lunged toward the parking lot. The sea breeze burnt his lungs as he gulped one ragged breath after another. He made his way across the parking lot, toward the Dumpster across the street. He gripped the front bar, squeezing as tightly as his hands would allow. Stutteringly, his mind began listing his surroundings. Garbage. Blue Dumpster. Gray gravel. He tried to remind himself he wasn't in that place anymore.

"Jake? Jake?"

A voice, soft and gentle, beckoned from the side of the confusion. He squeezed the Dumpster bar tighter, breathing in the stench of garbage, letting the pungency bring him back.

"Jake?" Suddenly the voice was closer and he felt a hand on his shoulder. The touch was tender, soothing. It promised comfort. Peace.

Somehow he managed to turn his head in the voice's direction.

"Are you all right? Did something happen?" Zoe was asking.

The sympathy in her pale blue eyes did more than any grounding technique. Reality crashed back, reminding him where he was and why.

Humiliation swept over him. "I'm fine," he said, pushing off both from the bar and her touch. "I needed some fresh air is all."

"In front of a garbage Dumpster?" She forced herself back into his line of vision. "Was it those two guys? I don't speak Spanish, but…"

"Portuguese. They were speaking Portuguese, not Spanish."

"All right, I don't speak Portuguese, either. Still, I could tell the news wasn't good. The look on Javier's face didn't look good."

"A car accident killed their friend."

Her hand flew to her lips. "My God. That's terrible. Did you know—?"

"No." His skin was clammy and cold. No, he didn't know the man, but he knew the loss. God, but he knew the loss. I just needed air," he lied again. "Stomach's bothering me."

"Are you sure?"

"I'm sure." His reply was rougher than necessary, but he didn't care. He could still feel the memory of Zoe's hand on his shoulder. That the sensation remained made his heart race, and not in a good way. He didn't deserve to feel anything, least of all comfort. "Let's just go back and ring up the supplies."

"The manager already is. He's going to load up his truck and drive us back to the dock."

Good. The sooner they got back, the sooner he could lose himself in work, which meant the sooner he could bury his thoughts.

Along with the sensation of Zoe's touch, still lingering on his skin.

What on earth had she witnessed?

One moment they were buying supplies, the next Jake was bolting for the door. Common sense told her to leave well enough alone. She had enough on her plate putting the pieces of her life back together without getting involved in someone else's problems. Only she'd never been very good at leaving anything alone. Not when someone might need her.

Besides, Jake hadn't said a word since they'd left the hardware store and the continual silence ate at her.

"Do you want to talk about it?" she asked when they'd finished transferring the supplies from Jake's boat to the back of his truck.

"Talk about what?"

"What happened back on the Vineyard? In the parking lot?"

"I told you—I needed fresh air."

"Right, and I'm tall enough to play professional basketball." She didn't buy his excuse for a second. Something had upset him—terrified him, nearly—and she was pretty sure it had to do with the conversation they'd overheard. "Were you in a car accident?"

The laugh he gave her was part amused, part mocking. "No," he replied, climbing into the driver's seat.

But he had been in some kind of accident. Those scars and that limp didn't appear by magic. Taking a page from his book, she stared straight ahead, pretending to watch the road rise over the bluff. "I only ask because sometimes hearing bad news can trigger—"

"Will you leave it alone?" The sharpness in his voice made her jump. "I wanted some air so I went outside. End of story. Now, for God's sake, would you let the subject drop?"

"I'm simply—"

He whipped around. "I said drop it!"

Suddenly Zoe understood. There, in the confines of his pickup, she saw what he hid beneath the layers of inapproachability.

Pain.

Not physical pain, like his hip. No, this kind of pain ran deeper and stronger. It was the kind of pain medicine couldn't help. The kind that ripped a man's insides apart.

Zoe's own insides hurt for him. "I'm sorry," she replied, meaning far more than her earlier intrusion.

She watched as he dragged a shaky hand across the back of his neck. Maybe it was her tone, or the fact that she'd apologized, but some of the edge left his voice. "I don't want to talk about it, okay?"

"Okay." She'd do what he wanted and let the subject drop. For now.

CHAPTER THREE

INSTALLING a dog run was harder than it sounded. For starters, pine trees didn't come with predrilled holes, meaning she had to figure out a way to attach the rope to the trunk. The easiest solution was to simply tie the rope around the trunk, but she couldn't get the knot tight enough. Her efforts kept sliding down to the ground, leaving her no choice but to screw a hook directly into the wood. Hopefully doing so wouldn't hurt the tree.

Jake would know whether it did or not, but she didn't want to ask. As it was, she felt amazingly self-conscious while she was working, convinced he was watching her miscues, and thinking her a royal idiot. No need to compound the situation with silly questions.

Her eyes strayed to the roof, where the handyman was busy attacking her chimney. Lovable chimney sweep from the children's movies he was not. He jammed the hard-bristled brush up and down with such fury, the creosote didn't stand a chance. Working out the pain from before, maybe? What was his story anyhow?

Beads of sweat had formed on the bridge of her nose, causing her glasses to slide. Taking them off, she wiped her damp skin with her sleeve. Man, but it was hot. She wasn't used to physical labor in the heat. If installing a doggy run counted as labor, that was. Still, she was hot and sticky. Jake had to be even stickier. He was working three times as hard and had yet to take a break.

"I'm grabbing a cold drink," she called up to him. "Do you want one?"

He shook his head and, after pausing briefly to wipe the sweat from his face, continued working.

"Talk about stubborn," Zoe said to Reynaldo. The dachshund was laid out dozing on the concrete step. "He wouldn't accept my offer of a drink while we were on the Vineyard, he wouldn't take one after his 'fresh air break,' and now he's still refusing. Either the man's impervious to heat or he wants to be hot and miserable." After today's events, she was leaning toward the latter.

"Well, I don't care how often he refused, he *has* to be thirsty. I am."

She grabbed two bottles of ice water from the kitchen fridge and made her way to the ladder propped on the side of the house.

When she reached the roof, she saw Jake had finished his chimney assault. He stood with his back

to her, breathing hard. Sweat and soot had turned
his light gray T-shirt dark and heavy. The material
stuck to his upper back like a dirty second skin. Zoe
couldn't help noticing the muscles underneath. She
was close enough that she could see the way they rippled like water every time he breathed deep. A wave
of female awareness coiled through her. Even standing still, he moved with grace. Her fingers twitched a
little as she wondered what the view might look like
beneath the cotton. Was it as hard and taut as the rest
of him?

Flushing, she cleared her thoughts and her throat.
"I decided to bring you a drink anyway."

His spine stiffened, and she could tell, despite
making noise, she'd startled him, making her feel
all the more like a voyeur for her earlier thoughts.
"Sorry. I didn't realize you were deep in thought.
Here."

"Do you always do what you want regardless of
what people tell you?"

Talk about a loaded comment. Thoughts of Paul
came to mind. "Unfortunately, yes. See, it's kind of
my job to know best. Ever hear of 'Ask Zoe'?"

"No."

She wasn't surprised. He didn't strike her as the
type to peruse the arts and lifestyle section. "It's a
nationally syndicated advice column. People write
in and ask me what they should do."

"And you tell them."

"That's the point of asking me, isn't it?"

"What if you're wrong?"

What if, indeed. "Anyway," she said, changing the subject, "as far as bringing you water, I prefer to use the term *executive overruling.* I don't need you getting light-headed from dehydration and falling off my roof."

Jake slipped the water from her hand. "Afraid of a lawsuit?"

"One big payout a year is enough, thank you."

As soon as the words left her mouth, she winced. Once again, she'd said too much. From the way Jake knit his brow, he must have caught her reaction as well. Shoot. Now she felt compelled to explain. "Expensive divorce. And before you say anything, yes, I'm aware of how ironic my situation sounds."

"Ironic?"

"A divorced advice columnist." She tried for a self-deprecating smile. "Guess I *can* be wrong sometimes."

She was grateful that Jake didn't reply; he was too busy draining his unwanted water bottle. Zoe tried not to notice the way his Adam's apple bobbed up and down with each swallow or how his biceps bulged from one simple bend of his arm.

Instead, she turned her attention to the shore across the street. There weren't many places where you could get a better bird's-eye view of the island.

Below them, Naushatucket spread out in beige, navy and green glory.

She scrambled up the last couple of rungs to get a better look, realizing only when she reached her destination how steeply pitched the Cape Cod-style roof was. Standing was awkward at best.

Pressing a hand to the chimney for support, she sat down. Across the street, the beach was mostly empty. The waves rolled gently toward them, their swells dark curves on the water's surface.

To her surprise, Jake lowered himself next to her. She could feel him looking at her. Zoe continued watching the waves. He'd spent the better part of the day ignoring her existence; she could do the same.

Except she hadn't counted on his attention making her skin twitch. Did the man always stare so intently? Even now, his gaze felt like it was looking inside her rather than at her.

"What?" she asked finally.

"Chimney's done," he replied. "You can use it tonight."

"Yay!" she cheered, although sitting in this heat, it was hard to remember why she'd needed a working fireplace to begin with.

She returned to studying the waves, the view turning her thoughtful. It didn't take long for those thoughts to become words. "There's something very centering about the islands, don't you think?"

"If you say so."

"Seriously. The idea of land, solid and strong, while surrounded by water. Can't get much more centered than that." Thoughts of her failures bubbled to the surface. "It's why I bought this place, you know. I was hoping some of that balance would rub off on me."

"How metaphysical of you."

"I take it you disagree with my theory."

Jake shrugged. "You can have any theory you want."

"From your tone, though, you don't believe a place can rub off on you."

"Rub off on you? Sure. But what you're talking about is a sense of peace." He raised the bottle to his mouth. "Big difference," he muttered over the rim. "Helluva big difference."

Zoe wondered if he meant for his sigh to be so long or so sad. She waited for him to go on, hoping for more explanation, but he simply tossed his empty water bottle over the edge of the roof. "Flashing around your chimney needs replacing," he said. "And you've got some loose shingles. Maybe even some soft spots in the wood."

Once again changing the subject. They were both, it appeared, quite adept at doing so. "That your way of telling me I need a new roof?"

"Depends," he replied with a shrug. "How badly do you want water leaking in?"

Short answer? She didn't. Neither did she relish

spending a lot of money on home repairs, which it looked like she was about to do. Damn her mother and Charles for not paying attention to this place.

It was her turn to sigh. "I don't suppose you know how to repair roofs."

"I've fixed one or two."

"Think you can fix this one?"

"Maybe."

Not the answer she wanted to hear. Why bring the darn repairs up, if he wasn't looking for the work?

Jake had pushed himself to his feet. Zoe immediately scrambled after him, except she lacked his innate grace and immediately began wobbling on the pitched slope. For the second time that day, a strong hand wrapped around her forearm, steadying her.

"Thank you," she murmured. Awareness had pooled at the spot where Jake's skin met hers. In the back of her mind, she noted that for a firm grip, his touch was surprisingly light and gentle. "Guess I won't be dancing on rooftops anytime soon," she said, attempting a smile.

The attempt wasn't returned. "You've got droppings," he said.

"What?"

"On the chimney. Probably bats."

Did he say bats? A shiver ran through her, and not the good kind of shiver, either. "Like in get-in-your-hair carry-rabies bats?" As if there were any other kind.

This time there was an attempted smile, or at least he quirked the corner of his mouth. "Afraid you'll have to mount another rescue mission?"

"Try attack. Are you sure there are bats?"

"Don't usually get guano otherwise."

And here she'd thought the swallow was her only pest problem. Bats? The very idea they could be living in her crawl spaces would keep her up all night. Turning her face to his, she mustered her best desperate expression. Not all that hard to do, seeing as she was desperate.

"Can you help me?" she asked him. "Please?"

The sigh Jake gave this time held an additional note. One that she swore sounded a lot like defeat. Zoe watched as he opened his mouth to speak, stopped and then looked down to where he still held her arm. The awareness flared anew. When he finally spoke, his voice was flat.

"I'll have to let you know."

She was waiting for a better answer; Jake could tell. But he was purposely ignoring the flash of orange perched on his ladder. If he looked, he would only find himself staring. It'd been happening all day. As long as she was near his line of sight, his eyes would find her. It was driving him mad. And the way his skin felt whenever he touched her, like it was alive... Well, he didn't like that, either.

So instead of looking, he forced his attention onto

the chimney. What he should have done was go home after that debacle in the store, but home would have only made his mood worse. When working he could bury the thoughts for a little while, 'til he collapsed in a heap of numbness and exhaustion. At least he used to be able to, before bright orange T-shirts and bouncy ponytails got in the way.

Why did he have to bring up the bats? Or the fact he was the only handyman on the island for that matter? Now, he was stuck. Only a coldhearted bastard could look at her face, with that quivering lower lip of hers, and say no. He had no choice but to help her now.

From below he could hear that damn dachshund yipping, followed by Zoe's admonishment to be patient. Sounded like the dog needed centering, too. Imagine thinking you could find peace by staying here on Naushatucket. If only it were that simple. Someone needed to tell her the truth: once you step on the wrong path, no amount of "balance" or redirection will make up for the distance you've already traveled. You can't go back. To use her word from this morning: life didn't come with do-overs.

Surprisingly, it wasn't the potential bat infestation dominating Zoe's thoughts the rest of the day, but the man sweeping her chimney.

On second thought, maybe it wasn't so surprising. After all, he'd been stuck in her head before the bat news; why wouldn't he stay there? Especially after hearing that long, sad sigh. The sound was now permanently merged with the memory of his expression outside the hardware store. So much pain and so many impenetrable layers. She wondered if anyone could ever get through them all to help.

"He's definitely a puzzle begging to be solved," she remarked to Reynaldo as they snuggled on the sofa later that night.

You're doing it again, the voice chimed. *Getting sucked in.* She couldn't resist a challenge any more than she could a sad story. Maybe if she could, she'd have seen the truth about Paul a lot sooner.

The fire in her newly cleaned fireplace crackled merrily, the flame painting the living room a soft orange. Yawning, Zoe tugged the comforter from off the back of the sofa and draped it over her and Reynaldo. A day of exertion in the sun had left her drowsy and more than a little stiff. She wondered how Jake's hip was doing. He'd been limping pretty badly when she saw him finally drag that ladder across the backyard.

Don't start, Zoe.

Her subconscious had a point. She had hundreds of readers looking for her advice. If she was desperate to solve other people's problems, she should focus on them, not the neighbor who had quite clearly told her to butt out.

Still, seeing the pain in those green eyes...

At some point she must have drifted off because before she realized it the pillow beneath her cheek was buzzing. Her cell phone, she realized drowsily. Probably Caroline, calling to nag her about this week's column. She never balked at calling at weird hours and the column was overdue.

"I'm working on it, Caroline," she barked into the transmitter. "No need to check in daily."

"You work too hard, babe."

Paul. Zoe nearly dropped the phone. She hadn't heard his voice in months. Not since she walked out. Hearing it now made her stomach drop.

Balling her free hand into a fist, she took a deep breath, willing her insides to still. "What do you want?" she managed to ask.

"Since when does a guy need an excuse to call his wife?"

"Ex-wife." Now she was over the shock, clarity was setting in. Thankfully. "I distinctly remember sending you papers. We're no longer married."

"I'll always think of us as married in my heart."

Didn't he mean wallet? "So much so you haven't tried to contact me since February."

"I wanted to give you your space."

"My space." He'd certainly given her that, and then some.

"Because I knew I screwed up." There was a pause. She imagined him chewing his thumb; he always did when nervous or deep in thought. "Truth is, I wasn't sure you'd talk to me."

"What makes you think I'm willing to talk with you now?"

He chuckled. "You answered the phone, didn't you?"

"Because I thought you were Caroline. I can still hang up, and I will, unless you tell me why you're calling."

"I miss you."

"I've been gone for months, Paul." He'd been gone even longer, but she doubted he'd understand what she meant.

Meanwhile, he ignored her comment. "I'm playing Savannah this weekend. Remember last year? The tenth hole? The water hazard?"

"I remember." She also remembered him sweet-talking her into ponying up for lessons with Lars Anderson afterward.

"We were good together, Zo."

"Were we?"

"Of course, we were. We were Team Brodsky."

Team Brodsky. She'd coined the silly moniker the night she proposed. At the time, Paul had been on the brink of making the tour. "Make me your partner," she'd said. "We can do great things together. Team Brodsky, all the way to number one." Her backing, his talent. That'd been the plan anyway.

"Ancient history," she said.

"Doesn't have to be." His voice dropped a notch, turning all honeyed and soft.

Once upon a time, that tone of voice would have sent her heart fluttering. Today it brought nothing but regret and bitterness.

"You were—you are—my lucky charm, babe. Always have been."

Not to mention his bankroll. She read the sports pages. He'd missed the cut in the last tournament. His short game was slipping without the expensive coach she'd been paying for.

On the other end of the line, there was another pause. More thumb-biting, she presumed. Finally he spoke again, clearly taking her silence as a willingness to listen. "What do you say? Can we at least talk? That's all I'm asking for. A chance to see you. I need you, Zoe."

And there it was, her Achilles' heel. *Need.* Forget sob stories and challenges. Never had there been a more powerful four-letter word, at least for her, and Paul knew it. Already she could feel the guilt building in her chest. Squeezing the phone, her nails bending against the plastic casing, she fought the emotion's grip. "I have to go."

"One meeting, Zoe. One."

"Goodbye, Paul."

She hung up before he could muster another argument, then quickly blocked his number from her phone before he could call again. And he would call again. Paul never liked rejection.

Dammit! She tossed the phone to the other end of the sofa, where it fell into the cushions. Why'd she have to answer the phone in the first place? Why didn't she take the time to look at the call screen?

It wasn't that she loved Paul. On the contrary, she was angry she had let herself be blinded by infatuation for as long as she did. Zoe Hamilton, Advice Columnist and Patsy. Tell her you need her, and you can walk all over her. Well, no more. Just like Team Brodsky, her days of becoming personally involved were history.

All of a sudden, her warm, cozy living room felt hot and stifling. To quote her neighbor, she needed some fresh air. Outside was still light enough that she could take a good brisk walk on the beach and clear her head.

"Come on, Rey." She nudged the sleeping dog. "Let's get out of here."

Grabbing the dachshund's leash, she headed out the patio door. Halfway through, she collided with a wall of muscle and bay rum.

"There a problem?" she heard Jake ask.

She had a problem all right. Her life. "I was taking Reynaldo for a walk."

Since leaving her, he'd showered and changed. His bangs hung wet against his forehead, and she noticed droplet stains on the collar of his work shirt. The top three buttons were undone, revealing an expanse of tanned skin and blond chest hair. To her mounting annoyance, he looked way too good.

He held up a flashlight and what looked like a fisherman's net. "I thought you wanted to tackle your bat problem."

Right, the bats. Dealing with her pest of an ex-husband had made her forget her house was potentially infested with rabid winged creatures. "And I thought you had to think about it?" she snapped back. Uncalled for? Yes. But he was staring at her in that intense way of his again, and she wasn't in the mood. She wasn't in the mood for anything right now except Reynaldo and a long walk on the beach.

If her neighbor noticed her sharpness, he was ignoring it. In fact, he matched her, edge for edge. "If you want to find where they're nesting, now's the time to look."

"So go look."

He thrust an industrial-size flashlight in her direction. "It's a two-person job."

Oh, great. Just what she wanted to do after a call from her ex. Go hunting for pests. Worse, she doubted her "handyman" would let her decline.

She snatched the flashlight from his hand. "Lead the way," she snapped. "Though, if I get rabies, I'm not paying you."

"They don't usually bite people. You're more likely to get rabies from a skunk than a bat."

"Well, aren't you the bat expert."

"Not an expert. Read up on them, is all."

Zoe blushed. The phone call had left her feeling churlish, and she was taking the feelings out on Jake instead of her ex-husband, which wasn't fair. Curmudgeon or not, he deserved better behavior from her.

She followed him around to the front of the house. "Up there's the area where I found the droppings," he explained. "Flashing's rippled on this side of the chimney, too. I'm guessing that's the point of entry."

In the dusk, Zoe could barely make out where he was talking about, despite the flashlight beam. The "ripple" he mentioned was barely big enough for a bee's nest. The netting, he explained, was to allow the bats to exit but not reenter. Then, after a week or so, they could plug the holes permanently.

Sounded good to Zoe. "What made you read up on bats in the first place?" she asked. Having been put in her place, she was trying to make amends. Plus, the comment had her curious.

"Spent a lot of time in caves. Figured knowing more about them would come in handy."

"Back where you grew up?"

"Afghanistan. Look, there she is." He pointed to a black dot zigzagging across the sky.

Zoe followed his finger, but her mind was more on his last answer than on her winged invader. It all made sense. The scars, the injury, the extreme reaction in the hardware store... How could she not have realized? Jake hadn't been in an accident. He'd been in battle.

"How long were you there?"

"Second one," he replied, ignoring the question. "Definitely coming out from the flashing. I'll have to check for sure, but it's early enough in the season that I don't think they've gotten through to inside the house."

"Good to know." Though she'd prefer to hear more about his military experience. "What am I out here for?"

"You're doing it. Keep the flashlight trained on the roof so I can see what I'm doing. Unless—" he glanced over his shoulder "—you'd rather wait 'til morning."

"Oh, no, tonight is fine. Sooner they're out of my hair...that is, my house," she corrected, "the better." Stepping closer to the ladder, she aimed the flashlight beam toward the roof. "Bright enough?"

"It'll do."

They worked in spotted silence. As clear as it was that Jake was in charge, he had a way about him that inspired her to obey his directions. Maybe it was the confidence of his commands or the surety of his movement. Or the way he told her what to do without pretense or a false front. Either way, they worked together so easily it took Zoe by surprise. She hadn't expected them to be such a good team.

Like Team Brodsky?

Giving herself a mental kick, she focused on shining her flashlight.

"Is that it?" she asked when he came down the ladder. "You're finished?"

"Doesn't take very long to plug a hole. By the way, I think they're all out of the nest, so you can sleep soundly."

"Thank goodness," she said with a sigh. "A warm, bat-free house." Sounded fantastic. "You, Jake Meyers, are my hero."

She couldn't have picked a worse thing to say. In the white glare of her flashlight, Zoe watched as his expression became a haunted, bitter mask.

"Don't ever use that word around me." He ground out the words through clenched teeth. "A hero is the last thing I am."

CHAPTER FOUR

OF ALL the terms Zoe could have used, why'd she have to pick the word *hero*? He could still see her face when she said it, too. Lit up like a kid at Christmas, her smile bright in the dark. The minute she grinned, he got a swell of male pride smack in the middle of his chest.

Jake slammed his beer on the TV tray that doubled as an end table. What right did he have to feel proud about anything, let alone be called a hero? Heroes sacrificed their lives, they saved lives.

Pushing himself from the sofa, he hobbled to his side window. Next door Zoe's house was dark, except for one lone window on the second floor. Her bedroom perhaps? Awareness shot to his groin, causing him to groan. He didn't want to feel this pull of attraction any more than he wanted to feel pride. Mere arousal he could deal with. After all, a man couldn't always help his physical reaction when an attractive woman crossed his path and he'd be kidding himself if he didn't admit Zoe was an attractive woman, in her spunky, wet-kitten kind of way.

This pull, though… All day long, his skin twitched, while his chest felt tight and empty at the same time. He didn't like the feeling. Didn't want the feeling. Hell, he didn't want to *feel,* period.

A cramp ran down the back of his leg. Climbing around all day had him stiff and achy. God, but it had been a long day. Between the nightmare and the flashback, not to mention all the physical labor, he should be ready to drop, and if it were any other night, he would. No such luck tonight. If anything, he was more restless than ever.

Looked like another long night of bad television. Relinquishing himself to his fate, he headed to the sofa, but not before taking one last look at the house next door. Zoe's window had gone dark.

He attributed the strange knot in his chest to beer and exhaustion.

It seemed like Zoe had just fallen asleep when her phone rang. With a groan, she reached over Reynaldo's sleeping body and grabbed the nightstand clock. Five-thirty. Good God.

"Good. You're awake." Caroline's voice was laced with coffee and cigarettes.

"No one's awake at this hour," she muttered. Closing her eyes, she burrowed back into her cave of blankets. "What do you want?"

"Your column."

Naturally. Zoe groaned again. "You know, I'm pretty sure your job title reads 'assistant.' As in assist, not browbeat."

"You hired me to keep you efficient. Which means making sure your column gets in on time. Which means browbeating. And since you've moved yourself to East God-knows-where—"

"Naushatucket."

"Whatever. You leaving the city means I have to start my browbeating extra early."

"Relax, Brunhilda, I still have two days."

"No, you have nine hours. Today's Wednesday, remember?"

"Crap." Panic replaced sleepiness and Zoe sat up straight.

"You forgot, didn't you?" Caroline said.

"I was busy with some house problems. I got distracted."

"House problems? Told you moving to nowhere was a mistake."

"You know, people in cities have house problems, too," Zoe replied. "It's what happens when you buy a house. Regardless, it's no big deal. I hired a handyman." A handyman whose extreme reactions and anguished expression had distracted her far more than anything else last night. Including Paul, she realized with a frown.

Don't ever use that word to describe me. The ache

in her heart that kept her up half the night started up again.

Meanwhile, on the other end of the phone, she could practically hear Caroline smirking over her latte. "Still upset I called so early?"

"Sadly, no." Truth was, for all her browbeating, Caroline was worth her weight in gold. During the worst days of her separation, when she was finding out more and more about Paul's infidelities, Caroline had also been her rock, patiently listening while she ranted and raved about the evils of falling in love with the people you're trying to help. "I'm glad one of us is on top of things."

"Okay, that doesn't sound good. What happened? I thought hiding out was supposed to get you back on your game."

"So did I." Zoe sighed.

"Give yourself time. It's only been a couple of days. Bet you're not even unpacked yet, are you?"

"Almost. I ran into a few home repair issues." Briefly she explained, ending with the story about the bats. "Now I've got these bat nets or whatever they are hanging off my roof. Jake said he'll check them for critters this morning."

"Jake?"

"The handyman I hired."

"Oh, right. I didn't realize you were on a first-name basis."

"This is a small island. Everyone's on a first-name basis."

"Uh-huh."

Again, Zoe could hear the smirk, this time accompanied by a healthy dose of innuendo. "For crying out loud, the ink's barely dry on my divorce. Last thing I'm interested in is another relationship. Besides, this guy's not exactly 'relatable,' if you know what I mean."

"He doesn't like girls?"

"He doesn't like people in general, I don't think." Saying the words brought a lump of sadness to her stomach. "He's got baggage." Too much baggage for one man to carry, she suspected.

"Uh-oh. Sounds like somebody's found a new project."

If only. "He's not looking for help, Caroline. In fact, the exact opposite," she added in a low voice. "I can't explain it, but I almost think he wants to suffer." *Don't ever use that word to describe me.* "He's punishing himself for something, only I don't know what."

"Let me guess. You're the only person who can understand him." More than a little sarcasm laced Caroline's voice. Zoe'd used that very line dozens of times when defending Paul.

"It's nothing like that," she replied. "And remember, friend or not, you can still be fired."

"No, I can't—your career would fall apart without me."

True, though she didn't need to sound so smug.

"Getting back to this handyman," Caroline continued. "Is he cute?"

"I'm not sure *cute* is the right word." She thought about how easily he moved around the roof. "More like very masculine."

"Nice. Break a pipe, then send me a photo of him in a wet T-shirt."

"Very funny. Seriously, this guy has some major issues. It's hard not to wonder what caused them."

"Well, while you're speculating, make sure you focus on getting that column done. Syndicators get very cranky when the content arrives late."

"Yes, boss. Anything else?"

"Yeah, keep your distance. I know you love a good sob story and all…"

Caroline wouldn't say that if she'd seen Jake's eyes. Still, Zoe reassured her. "I have absolutely no intention of repeating past mistakes. My bank account can't afford it."

After going over a few more business details, Zoe hung up and headed downstairs. Thanks to Caroline, going back to sleep was impossible.

Reynaldo came trotting into the kitchen behind her, yawning. Even half asleep, Zoe had to giggle. If dogs could have bedhead, he definitely qualified.

"What do you say we take that walk on the beach we never got to last night?"

Sensing potential freedom, the dachshund perked up with a bark.

This time of morning, the two-mile strip of sand was close to empty. The sun had barely breached the horizon, a large orange-pink half circle that promised another warm day once the pockets of fog burned away. The air smelled of water and salt. Taking a deep breath, Zoe allowed the aroma to wash over her. Yes, she thought, time on the beach was exactly what she needed.

How on earth had her life gotten to this place? Eight months ago she'd been on top of the world. Now here she was, paying support to a philandering husband and living next door to an enigmatic handyman she couldn't get out of her head.

Ever the nudge, Reynaldo whined and pulled on his leash. "Chill, Reynaldo. I don't care how wide open the space is, you need to stay on the leash."

The dachshund whined again. There were birds about and he clearly wanted to chase them. Sighing, she looked up and down the deserted beach. The only people that she could see were two die-hard fishermen casting into the surf.

"You're a spoiled brat, you know that, don't you?"

He took off the second she unhooked his leash.

Free from the confines of his harness, he embarked on a quest to rid the beach of seagulls.

"At least he's not chasing chipmunks."

Hearing Jake's voice, she started. Her neighbor was making his way along the shoreline. He must have come from around the rocks behind her because she hadn't seen him earlier.

Based on the foam cup he held in his hand, she guessed he'd walked to the diner in town. He was wearing a pair of snug, torn jeans and a gray sweatshirt dotted with paint. An equally ragged Boston baseball cap topped his head, and his shoes were covered with sand.

He looked sexy as all get out.

Suddenly Zoe regretted her decision to walk in her flannel pajamas. Combing her hair into something more than a sloppy ponytail would have been nice, too. She quickly undid the tie from her hair and refastened it, hoping she looked nonchalant as she did so.

"Give him time," she quipped. "The day's still early."

His face didn't react to the joke.

She continued, "I didn't know anyone else would be up this early. The sunrise is gorgeous, isn't it?"

In the last minute the sun had risen another inch above the water, bringing its color to more of the sky. "There's something about the light breaking through the gray that makes me feel inspired to tackle the day."

"Makes me think it's early. And that I should be asleep."

Yet he wasn't. In fact, had he slept at all? Given his dark circles and haggard appearance, she wondered.

As soon as Reynaldo realized she had a companion, he took a break from his bird-chasing duties and ran up to them. Rather, he ran up to Jake. Jumping up and down, he barked incessantly as though greeting a long-lost friend.

Jake scowled. "What is with this dog?"

"Apparently he likes you."

"Lucky me."

"Either that or he thinks you've got food. Rey's two biggest motivators are his appetite and his bladder."

"Glad to see he's got the important things down."

Oh, Lord, was that an attempt at humor she heard tripping off his lips? Zoe felt the corners of her mouth tug upward. "No one can accuse him of not having his priorities in order, that's for certain," she said.

Proving her point, Rey turned his attention away from Jake, and promptly trotted to a nearby scrub of beach grass, where he relieved himself. "My assistant, Caroline, calls him my substitute child because I cater to him so much," she remarked.

"She might have a point," Jake replied.

Adjusting her glasses as camouflage, she took a look at her companion. He was sipping his coffee, his green eyes focused on the frolicking dachshund. Again, she was struck by the fatigue and sadness hovering around him. Even standing here with her and Reynaldo, he looked alone. Alone and far away.

"I'd wanted a pet forever." She hoped that sharing might draw him out. "When I was a kid, we couldn't have a pet—my dad had breathing issues—so as soon as I got a place of my own I headed straight for the pound. Believe it or not." She chuckled. "I'd planned on getting a retriever."

"And instead you got the tube of terror."

"Tube of terror?"

"Couldn't think of a *T* word that means annoying," he replied with a shrug.

Zoe laughed. "Reynaldo, tube of terror. Suits him."

Jake's mouth quirked upward, the closest he'd come to a smile since she met him. Seeing it brought more warmth than the rising sun. "So, from retriever to dachshund. How'd that happen?"

"Couldn't help myself. Every time I walked past the cage, he would whimper and look at me with his sad brown eyes. Then the woman at the shelter told me he'd been found abandoned and left tied up behind a drugstore. Soon as I heard that, I was hooked. I've always been a sucker for a good sob story."

"Either that or Reynaldo is a master manipulator."

"You might be right." She was a sucker for those, too. "Anyway, I couldn't stand the idea of the little guy not having a home."

"I'm surprised you were so keen on outing the bats then. Seeing as how you've blocked them from their nests."

"That's different. That was self-preservation. Although..." She frowned. "I didn't think about the fact I was rendering them homeless. Do you think they sell bat houses at the hardware store?"

His head tilted like a questioning puppy, Jake studied her. "You really would buy one, wouldn't you?"

"I booted them from their nest. Shouldn't I help to fix their problem?"

"Do you always feel compelled to solve problems?"

"Sure," Zoe replied, undoing and fixing her ponytail again. She was painfully aware of his eyes sweeping her length, his evaluation spreading through her limbs like honey. She shrugged, affecting nonchalance. "See a problem, try to help. Advice columnist, remember?"

"I remember." He took a long drink from his coffee, silence swirling around him like the ocean breeze. "What if you can't help?"

Was he talking about himself? They sure weren't

talking about bats anymore. There was such resignation in his voice as he spoke, it hurt.

"Not every problem can be fixed," he continued.

"I don't believe that," she countered. "Every problem can be fixed, with time."

"Well, that's why you're the advice columnist and I'm not." Before she could reply, he started walking toward the street. Whatever crack he'd allowed in his armor was sealed once more. "I'll go check your roof to see if any bats got left behind last night. Good luck getting that dog back on a leash."

"If I can't, I'll simply wave a doggy biscuit. Never underestimate the lure of food."

He shot her another half smile, and went on his way.

How long she stood watching the waves, Zoe didn't know. Could have been an hour or a few minutes. The inner peace she'd hoped to find never materialized. She felt off-kilter. Out of sorts. More so than before, if possible. The sadness that laced Jake's voice continued to hang in the air, thick and unrepentant.

What was it about the man that his presence surrounded her even after his departure? Why couldn't she stop thinking about him?

Suddenly her thoughts were cut by the sound of a horn blasting in the morning air. Zoe heard the screech of tires followed by a high-pitched yelp.

Reynaldo. Her eyes searched the dunes looking for him, only to have her stomach sink with dread.

The dachshund was nowhere in sight.

No, no, no. Sand spraying behind her, she took off for the street. *Please, no. Not Reynaldo.* Why had she let him off the leash? Why hadn't she paid closer attention? Stupid, stupid daydreaming. She scrambled over the top ridge onto the street.

A gray sedan was pulled to the side of the road and a pair of elderly fishermen were standing next to it. When they saw her, one of them came rushing over.

"We didn't see him 'til he was in front of the car. Ran right out in the street, he did."

Oh, God, no. Not Rey. She pushed past the man, dreading what she was about to see, only to stop dead in her tracks.

There, legs sprawled in the gravel, sat Jake, his arms wrapped around a very much unscathed Reynaldo.

"We were headed down to the point when the dog darted into the street. If this guy hadn't grabbed him, we would have hit the little guy for sure."

Gratitude—along with a healthy dose of admiration—swelled in Zoe's chest. She wanted to speak, but the words, along with her heart, seemed stuck in her throat, so she settled for kneeling down beside him. Reynaldo squirmed in Jake's grip. Whether out of excitement or from knowing he'd narrowly escaped injury, the dog was bent on licking his savior's chin, a gesture Jake was receiving rather unenthusiastically.

"Calm down, Rey." She'd finally found her voice, albeit it was not much more than a whisper. Gently, her hands shaking, she slipped the dog from Jake's grip. "Are you all right?" she asked Jake.

"Are you talking to me or the dog?"

"You." His gruffness made her smile. "Are you hurt?"

"I'm fine."

"Thank God," one of the fishermen said. Zoe could tell from his tone he'd feared otherwise and was grasping at Jake's answer like a life preserver. "You went down pretty hard when my fender clipped you."

The car struck him? Zoe's eyes shot up to meet Jake's, only to find his expression shuttered.

"I said I'm fine." He moved to push himself up, only to grimace with pain and sit back down.

"You're not all right at all," Zoe said. She shifted Reynaldo to her hip, and reached for him with her now free hand. "Your hip—"

"Zoe, I don't want your help! Just go take care of your damn dog and leave me alone."

Her insides recoiled, but not from Jake's verbal slap. Though harsh, his words were nowhere near as painful as watching him struggle to hide his embarrassment while he accepted a hand up from the fishermen. It took all her effort not to reach out and reassure him when he reached his feet. She stood in silence, arms wrapped around Reynaldo as he nodded a curt thank-you to the men and limped toward his front yard.

"What about your leg?" one of the men called out, only to be waved off.

The driver turned to Zoe. "I honestly didn't see either of them."

"It's not your fault," Zoe replied. "I should have been paying closer attention myself but I got distracted." *Distracted by thoughts of Reynaldo's savior.*

Thoughts that filled her mind with even greater ferocity as she watched him disappear through his front door.

CHAPTER FIVE

Dear Zoe

My boyfriend of three years refuses to talk about marriage. Whenever I bring up the topic, he laughs and says he hasn't "made up his mind yet." My friends tell me I should break up with him, but I'm afraid I won't meet anyone else... I'm overweight and not very pretty.

Ugly in New York

Dear Ugly

If your boyfriend hasn't "made up his mind" in three years, I'm not sure he ever will. More importantly, however, why are you so certain he's your only shot at happiness? Don't be so down on yourself! I'm willing to bet you have far more to offer than you give yourself credit for. My advice: dump the loser and find some-one who appreciates you.

Zoe

OKAY, "dump the loser" was probably over the top. She'd end with "give yourself credit for."

Hmm. Reminded her of someone else who didn't give himself enough credit. Lord, but her stomach still churned thinking of how close she had come to losing her precious Reynaldo. If not for Jake…

And he didn't want to be called a hero.

Following Rey's rescue, she'd tried to discourage her handyman from working. As far as she was concerned, her loose shingles could wait a day or two. His hip had to be killing him. But no sooner did she make the suggestion than he'd snapped back, "I said I'd start your roof today so I'm doing it," and hobbled up the ladder.

She could hear him up there now, scraping off shingles. He'd draped a plastic blue tarp around the entire house. It blocked her view and filled every room with dark blue shadows and every five minutes or so, debris would rattle down the plastic like heavy rain. Six and a half hours and he'd yet to take a break, at least not one she'd heard. Like yesterday, he seemed intent on working 'til he dropped. Zoe could picture him up there, muscles straining, sweat dampening his shirt. His face contorting every time he moved…

Well, she decided, pushing the laptop aside, the very least she could do was make sure the man who saved Reynaldo took a lunch break. She still couldn't believe he'd jumped in front of that car. Without him her sweet little dog would be...

Lump sticking in her throat, she paused to pet the dachshund sleeping next to the sofa.

Yeah, she thought, lunch was the least she could do.

Since getting Jake to come down and join her was unlikely, she decided to bring the food to him. Fortunately she'd brought a small beach cooler with her when she moved. She filled it with turkey sandwiches, fruit and cold drinks. As an afterthought, she included a bottle of ibuprofen, and stepped outside.

To her surprise, the sky was far from sunny when she stepped out of her blue-shaded cave. While she'd been inside, her bright cheery sun had been replaced by a collection of gray clouds. Even so, the air felt warm and thick when she reached the top of the ladder. Jake was leaning against his shovel, eyes closed. She'd been right about the sweat. His T-shirt was soaked. The cotton molded across his shoulders and broad chest before falling loose over his flat abdomen.

Zoe's throat ran dry.

"Knock, knock," she said hoarsely.

He started and briefly, when his eyes widened, she worried he might lose his balance. A silly concern, she realized soon enough as he quickly steadied himself. His lips drew into a tight line. He wasn't happy to see her.

Zoe held up her minicooler. "Greetings. I come bearing food. It's lunchtime, in case you haven't noticed."

An unreadable expression crossed his features. "You don't have to feed me."

"Of course I do. Reynaldo would never forgive me, seeing as how food is his life and you saved his life. Which reminds me…" She set the cooler down and eased herself onto the peak, careful not to slip on the exposed wood. "In case I didn't say it before, thank you."

Jake shrugged. "Dog ran into the street—I grabbed him."

"It's a little bigger deal than that," Zoe said. If she didn't think he'd balk at the word, she'd call him a hero again. "I would have lost my best friend today if it weren't for you." She offered up a grateful smile, which he didn't return.

He did, however, meet her eyes. "I'm glad you didn't. No one should have to lose a friend."

Had he? Something about his voice, hollow and sad, made her shiver.

A heavy silence settled between them. Zoe forced herself to look away. "Hope you like turkey on white. One of those women who can whip up a gourmet meal at the drop of a hat, I'm not. Takeout is more my forte. You have no idea how thrilled I was to learn they opened a restaurant near the ticket office."

Jake rubbed the back of his neck. "Not sure I'd

call the 'Tucket a restaurant. More like a glorified greasy spoon."

"Hey, it serves food I don't have to cook—that makes it a five-star restaurant in my book. Now, come sit down and eat your lunch."

Jake was staring at the sandwich she'd thrust in his direction.

"Don't worry, it's edible. I promise."

Carefully, he lowered himself down next to her, his grimace a reminder of how much a personal toll Rey's rescue had taken on him. Reaching into the cooler, Zoe pulled out the bottle of ibuprofen. "Thought you might want this, too."

Jake shook his head. "Won't help."

"Not even a little?"

"Nothing does."

Nothing?

"I've got some prescription stuff at home, but that more dulls it than anything."

His matter-of-factness amazed her. She couldn't imagine living with continual pain, and that fact made what he'd done this morning even more impressive. She wanted to say so but the edge in his voice made her hold back. She settled for a soft murmur of sympathy.

"Stuff happens when you catch a mortar shell," he replied with his typical shrug. As if people caught mortar shells every day.

Dear Lord. "You're lucky you weren't killed."

Jake stared at his sandwich. "So they tell me."

Again, his hollow voice made her shiver.

They continued eating their sandwiches in silence. Part of Zoe wanted to fill the quiet with idle chitchat, but another, more sensible part made her bite her tongue and study the seascape. A line of weather was working its way across the water. To the right, on the edge of shingling, a piece of white string caught her eye. The netting from last night.

"How goes the bat hunting?" she asked. "Find any more winged creatures of the night?"

"No." Was that a half smile teasing his cheek? Tentative as it was, the sight raised Zoe's spirits. "Not so far anyway. The valves were empty—"

"Valves?" she interrupted.

"The netting we installed last night. It was empty and I haven't seen any additional signs of damage. I'll check the attic to make certain, but I'd say you lucked out. You still serious about getting a bat house?"

"Absolutely." Seemed only right. "Bats are people, too, right?"

For whatever reason, the answer met with his approval, because he nodded. "I admire your conscientiousness."

Really? "You do?"

"You sound surprised."

"To be honest, I am," she told him. "I got the impression you think I'm a bit of a flake."

He regarded her. "Not flaky. Hyper-helpful, but not flaky."

"Thank you. I guess." A bit backhanded, perhaps, but he clearly meant it as a compliment. The warmth flooding her cheeks suggested she certainly took it as one.

Goodness, but she didn't get this man. Gruff one minute, reluctantly nice the next—although she suspected he would insist niceness had nothing to do with anything. She could hear Caroline scoffing now, but how could a woman—that is, a person—not meet Jake and be intrigued?

Before she could dwell too long, her thoughts were interrupted by a splash of water landing on her cheek. Then another, followed by another. Looking out to the ocean, she saw the rain line had drawn closer.

"So much for a picnic. Looks like we'll have to finish inside." Without waiting for a response, she plucked Jake's half-eaten sandwich out of his hand. He looked about to protest when the drops started to fall faster. Together they scrambled to pick up the tools and food before the rain moved in.

They didn't make it. In fact, Zoe had barely stepped off the bottom ladder rung when the sky opened up and what had been isolated drops became a steady downpour.

No sooner did they fight their way through a gap in the blue tarp and enter the living room than Reynaldo, annoyed at being left behind, began yelping and dancing circles. Just as he had this morning on the beach, he lavished most of his attention on Jake.

"Reynaldo, heel!" Like the command would do any good. Tongue out, tail wagging, the little dog was practically doing back flips trying to get Jake to notice him.

A giggle bubbled up in Zoe's chest. She didn't know which was more amusing: Reynaldo's desperate ploy or the exaggerated scowl on Jake's face.

"Looks like someone likes you," she said.

"Well, tell him to stop."

"Too late, I'm afraid. Once Rey makes up his mind about a person, nothing will shake him. Like a dog with a bone."

"Ha, ha."

"Seriously. He hated my ex-husband on sight. Used to growl at him. We had to keep him downstairs the nights Paul was home." You'd think she'd have picked up on the hint.

"Anyway—" she shook off the thought "—you might as well get used to having Reynaldo as your new best friend."

"I don't want friends, canine or other."

With that, Jake moved toward a large leather Barcalounger that used to be her father's favorite chair, and propped himself on the arm. "I'll take my sandwich back."

Zoe reached into the cooler and handed it to him.

"You say you don't want friends, and yet you saved mine."

"Told you, right place, right time, is all."

No, he'd told her no one should have to lose a friend. Strange thing to say for a man who didn't want any himself.

The blue-shaded room cast a different kind of shadow over his features, turning his face almost as gray as the weather outside. The lines marking his face were especially apparent today. Without meaning to, she let her gaze follow the longest one down his forehead to his brow. As prominent as these marks on his skin were, she had a feeling the scars below the surface were deeper and far more brutal.

He must have felt her stare because he turned to face her. "What?"

Aw, hell. In for a penny, in for a pound, right? "Was he a good friend?"

"Was who?"

Feigned ignorance wasn't his strong suit, but Zoe played along. "The friend you lost. On the roof, you said no one should lose a friend. That was obviously from personal experience. Were the two of you close?"

His expression remained passive. On the surface, it would look like he didn't react to what she said, but Zoe had been watching. She saw the subtle clench of his jaw as he swallowed his emotions. That said it all.

"I can only imagine what you must have felt," she continued.

Still no reply. He was wrapping himself up the way he'd wrapped the house. "If you ever want to talk…" she began.

"No." Finally he spoke. The word burst out of him like a shot, contorting his face with a distress so stark Zoe's heart hurt.

Right. That's why his eyes had darkened and unspoken words hung in the air around him. She crossed the room to sit on the chair next to him. "Look—" her fingers rested on the curve of his wrist "—I'm no therapist, but keeping things inside isn't healthy for anyone."

"Spare me the platitudes—I'm not one of your readers looking for advice."

Ouch. "You're right. You're not."

"And I don't want your help."

"I know that, too."

Yet she couldn't seem to help herself. His torment called out for help. She could hear it. Feel it. Why else would her heart be twisting in her chest?

"My question is, what do you want?"

"I—" Their eyes locked and his words faded away. The air, which had already felt thick and portentous, shifted. To Zoe, it felt like the warmth had seeped inside her. A heady, intoxicating feeling, it was the kind that gave birth to dangerous notions. But she couldn't pull away. Jake's eyes held her. And when he dropped his gaze to her mouth...

Then suddenly, the sensation disappeared, erased by the electronic sounds of jazz. As Jake fished his cell phone from his pocket, Zoe turned away, putting the distance back between them.

Behind her, Jake swore, the curse mild in volume only.

"Bad news?" She looked at her fingers. They were trembling.

"It's nothing." She didn't have to see his face to know the answer was a lie, and a bad one to boot, but she let it slide.

A couple beats passed. She imagined him studying the call screen on his phone. "You asked what I wanted," he said finally.

She turned back around. "Yes, I did."

"What I want is to be left alone."

Of course he did.

"What's so funny?"

Funny? Zoe realized she was chuckling aloud at the predictability. "Nothing." Her turn to lie poorly. "I couldn't help but wonder if that's your polite way of saying, stop asking questions."

"Nothing polite about it. Look," he asserted, pre-empting her when she opened her mouth to respond, "it's not personal. I don't... Relationships are no longer on my radar."

"I understand." Another poor lie. In truth, a

man like Jake shutting himself off didn't feel right. Especially when instinct told her that hadn't always been the case.

Still, now was not the time to push the point.

"Tell you what," she said. "From now on we're strictly handyman and home owner. No more personal questions."

Emotion flickered in the depths of his eyes. He was surprised that she agreed so easily, no doubt. "Thank you."

"No problem. For what it's worth, I recently made a similar vow myself."

"That so?" Now he definitely looked surprised.

"Surely you didn't think you'd cornered the market on wanting solitude, did you?"

"No." He regarded her for a moment. "Your divorce was more than expensive."

More of a statement than a question, Jake's comment brought with it a surprising feeling of understanding.

"It came with a lot of costs," she said.

"Doesn't everything?"

They looked at each other with nothing but the pitter-patter of rain on the tarp filling the room. Zoe tried to read his expression, but failed. Whatever thoughts were running through that handsome head, they remained hidden from the world.

"Do you want a second sandwich?" she asked at

last. He hadn't finished the first, but Zoe couldn't think of another excuse to speak.

"No, but thank you." Pushing himself to his feet, he stumbled slightly and fell forward, catching his footing a few inches from where she stood. The aroma of bay rum and masculinity wrapped itself around her body. Hooded eyes looked down at her, finding her mouth again.

"I—I should be going," he said. "Thank you for the sandwich."

She waited until he'd slipped around the blue tarp before letting out the long breath she didn't realize she'd been holding. "You're welcome."

The rain moved in for the rest of the day.

For a long time after Jake's departure, Zoe stood in the living room staring at the doorway, as if he might walk back in. He didn't.

Eventually she returned to the work waiting for her. While she still didn't feel like she had answers, her looming deadline left her little choice but to write something. Hopefully her readers would find her advice passable even if she didn't.

Outside, the blue tarp waved and buckled. Heading into the kitchen, she saw Jake pulling the plastic sheeting away from her windows. His hair and clothes were wet. Every so often he'd wipe the rain from his face.

Surely he didn't have to remove the plastic right

now. She could live with a shrouded house. Her eyes traveled to the coffeemaker.

No, he was out there because he wanted to be. She'd already trotted out once today with that silly picnic. She was not going to act like some smitten groupie or beg for his attention. If Jake wanted to be left alone, she would honor his request.

Instead, she poured a cup of coffee, returned to her laptop and focused her attention on the people who wanted it.

The plastic sheet rippled in the wind, making ma-neuvering difficult, but Jake eventually wrangled it under control. He didn't have to pull the tarp back; tomorrow he would only have to put it back into place. Through the living room window he saw Zoe on the sofa, typing away on her laptop. Her hair hung around her face. Every so often she'd comb it back from her eyes. His eyes traveled to the Barcalounger, his mind harkening back to her body swaying close to his. She'd smelled like lemons. Would her skin taste like them, too? The therapist at the VA used to suggest sucking on lemons to anchor himself during a flashback. *What do you want, Jake?*

No. He wouldn't go there. He'd meant what he said, about wanting to be left alone. He didn't want Zoe bopping up his ladder with sandwiches. He didn't want to "talk" with her or think of her as anything but the woman who hired him.

So instead he stood in the rain and wrestled with the plastic tarp, letting the rain cool his overheated skin.

The next morning, Zoe found herself still decidedly not thinking about her neighbor as she made her way to the hardware store to order a bat house.

"Take a couple days," Ira told her. "We don't stock 'em in the store. You mind?"

Zoe shook her head.

"Good to know. Some people aren't so patient about waiting." He grabbed an order pad from underneath the counter. "By the way, you find that handyman of yours?"

He's not mine, Zoe thought. *He's not anybody's.* Then she realized what the manager meant. "If you're talking about Jake, he's at my house scraping shingles off the roof as we speak."

His dark figure had appeared on her roof just after dawn. Zoe had *not* studied him through her rearview mirror as she drove away. "In fact, he's the reason for the bat house. He found some droppings."

"Good man. Does good work. I've hired him myself more than once."

Zoe couldn't help herself. "You know Jake well?"

"As well as anyone on the island I suppose. He's pretty private. Keeps to himself." He cast an eye at her over his order pad. "Why do you ask?"

"Curious, is all," she replied. Seemed like too vague a word, but she couldn't think of a better one.

"Well, like I said, he's a pretty private person. I'm sure he's got a good reason."

Meaning she'd get no more information from him. "Yes, I'm sure he does."

To be honest, she understood the reticence. The small year-round community naturally would be protective of one another, especially when it came to newcomers like her. Then again, it was possible, given Jake's barriers, Ira knew as little about her handyman as she did.

Her handyman. Second time today the phrase crossed her brain. Like before, she immediately issued a correction. Jake didn't belong to anyone. Especially her. Not that she wanted him to belong to her anyway.

There was no silhouette on the rooftop when she pulled into her drive, only tar paper and bare wood. She parked the car and headed toward the backyard, where she swore she could hear Reynaldo barking. Rounding the corner, she saw Jake attaching the dachshund to his dog run. Her stomach fluttered at the sight.

Because he was being nice to Reynaldo, not because she was relieved he hadn't left.

Rey was doing his usual circling and pirouetting around Jake's legs. "Hold your horses," he was saying. "Let me get you clipped up. There. Go bother the chipmunks for a little while instead of me." With a sharp bark, Rey trotted off toward the back end of the yard.

"See he's got you trained, too," she said, announcing her arrival.

He turned, causing the sunlight to hit his face just right, and light up his eyes like emeralds. Brilliant beyond belief, they somehow managed to look sad and wary at the same time. The effect shot straight through to her heart, and she felt a tiny lurch. He might not want friends, but she was looking at the eyes of a man who needed them.

"Deliveryman came and he started barking his head off," he said. "Wouldn't stop 'til I took him outside."

"He hates being left out of the action. Don't you, you spoiled brat?"

Too involved with sniffing tree roots, the dachshund didn't reply. "Of course," she continued, "now that he's out here with us, he'll ignore us."

"Proof things aren't always what they seem."

What was that odd statement supposed to mean? Cocking her head, she gave him a long, questioning look, hoping for an answer, but his face remained, like always, a sphinxlike mask.

Suddenly, something he said hit her. "Did you say I got a delivery?" Couldn't be the bat house. Probably a package from Caroline. Some item her assistant deemed vital to quality living no doubt, like an espresso maker or a big fat sign emblazoned with her deadline dates.

Jake answered without intonation. "On the back step."

Zoe looked. Then looked again to make sure she saw correctly. Sure enough, a floral arrangement in shades of pink sat by the back door. She'd been so focused on Jake and Reynaldo, she hadn't noticed.

A pretty amazing feat given the arrangement's size. The thing was huge. An over-the-top array of roses, calla lilies and delphinium, the kind of bouquet you'd send when trying to impress. Zoe knew only one person who would make such a grand-scale gesture. She slipped the card from its small white envelope.

Need you forever. Love, Paul

"I didn't know the island had a florist," she murmured. The lame comment was all she could muster. How had he known where to find her? Certainly not from Caroline.

"Doesn't. Came over on the ferry from the mainland."

Paul certainly had outdone himself. She'd never seen such an amazing arrangement. The roses were as big as her fist. Her finger traced a pale pink petal. Such a beautiful, delicate flower.

Too bad he wasted his money.

Picking up the arrangement, she walked over to the side of her garage.

And dropped the bouquet in the trash.

CHAPTER SIX

HER scalp tingled. Jake stood behind her, staring down. She waited for his comment, his question, whatever. After all, not every day did you get to see a woman trash a three-hundred-dollar floral arrangement.

He said nothing.

"I'm going for a walk," she announced, turning abruptly. She needed fresh air to clear away the scent of roses.

Unlike the early morning when only a handful of people dotted the shore, the beach at this time of day was full. Or as full as it could be prior to tourist season. At the public end of the strip, the morning's fishermen had been replaced by a line of multicolored umbrellas and beach towels. Mothers watched toddlers build sand castles. The sound of radios drifted on the wind.

Zoe headed to her left, where the rocks from the jetty formed a tiered tower. Part way up, they flattened, creating a large overhang. It was here she settled, leaning back and letting her legs over the edge. Beneath her feet, the waves crashed over smaller rocks, white foam bubbling into tide pools.

"Hey."

Looking up, she saw Jake approaching, a mug of coffee in his hands. "Took a coffee break," he said.

With impressive agility, he ascended the rocks and joined her. Handing her the mug, he settled himself on the rock next to her. When he was settled, she attempted to hand the cup back, only to have him shake his head.

"Thought you said you took a coffee break."

"I did. Didn't feel like drinking coffee is all."

But he'd brought her one. Gratitude, and something else—something stronger—built inside her. She took a sip, hoping it would push away the thickness in her throat. "Funny, I remember these rocks being much taller when I was little," she said.

"Things always look different when we're kids."

"True." She stared into her mug. "Aren't you going to ask?"

"Ask what?"

"Why I threw away the flowers."

"Figured you didn't like pink."

If he meant the remark to cheer her up, it worked; she smiled. Of course he wouldn't ask. She should have realized.

"They were from my ex-husband," she told him anyway. Since they'd met, she'd overshared. Why stop now? "He must have gotten my address from my mother. Lord knows how, since she never liked him. Said his teeth were too white."

Jake's brow knit in confusion.

"He's a golf pro," she continued with a shrug, as if that would explain. "At least, he tries to be. He claims he can't make it on the tour without my support. I caught him sleeping with a cocktail waitress at one of the tournaments. I'm pretty sure she wasn't the first. Guess my support wasn't enough."

Or she wasn't enough. The silent fear that continually plagued her subconscious made its way to the forefront of her thoughts. She tried to laugh it off, but the noise came out more a squeaky sigh. "My own fault really. Like I told you yesterday, I'm a sucker for sad stories. But—" she raised the cup to her lips for another sip "—not anymore. From here on in, I ride solo. I won't get used again."

"Wise decision."

Says the man who swore off the world. "Thank you."

Spray from the waves splashed across her ankles, dampening her jeans. The sudden splatter of cold on her skin made her yelp. It took some getting used to the New England waters. Damn stuff didn't warm until July or August, if it warmed at all.

"What's this place like in the winter?" she asked Jake.

"Thinking of hiding here year-round?"

The idea had merit, this morning anyway. "Wondering, is all."

"Cold," he replied. "Raw. Most of the businesses close up except for the hardware store and a couple others. You can go days without seeing another person."

"Sounds..." She was about to say "lonely," but realized the isolation was what he wanted. The idea of him holed up alone all winter shouldn't upset her, but it did.

Knowing any commentary would be unwelcome, she went back to studying the tide pool. From her perch she could see the ripples left by small fish as they snacked on algae.

"Look," she said, catching sight of five spiny rays out of the corner of her eye, "a sea star. I've never seen one up close before. Not outside an aquarium."

"According to the fishermen, there's been an increase in numbers the last couple years. I gather they're not happy to see them around."

"They may not be, but I am. I'm going to get a closer look." Setting down her coffee, she slipped off her sandals and slid downward, searching with her toes until she found purchase. After a few tries, she finally found a small rock an inch or so above the water she could lower down onto. Unfortunately, her stepping stone could only accommodate one foot so she was forced to balance on one leg.

"This might be harder than I thought," she said.

"Been a while since my gymnastics days. My center of gravity's not what it used to be."

"Looks fine to me."

The blush that shot down from her head to her toes did not help her balance. Surely he didn't mean the comment *that* way. Glancing up in his direction, she saw no indication in his expression that would refute the thought.

To cover her reaction, she kept talking. "My specialty was tumbling. Coach said I had powerful legs. Which was a polite way of saying I couldn't keep still. Ants in my pants, my mother used to say."

Steadying herself with one hand, she slowly crouched down. "Will you look at this beauty?" she said, lifting the yellow-orange creature to get a better look at the suckers on its underside. "The summer we stayed here, my dad and I would go scavenging on the beach. I got very good at finding dismembered crab claws and empty skate cases."

"Priceless items to a little girl," Jake said from above.

"Exactly. I had a whole treasure chest filled with booty. Well, a shoebox full anyway. Those were fun times." She tried—and failed—to keep a note of melancholy from slipping into her voice.

"How old were you when you stopped coming?"

"Seven. My father got sick that winter. We only got to spend one summer." From then on, life became about staying out of the way and not being a burden. *Settle down, Zoe. You're not helping.*

"We didn't get to do a lot of things," she said in a low voice. A chill ran up her leg. She blamed the cold water.

"We didn't live near the beach, but our town had a pool. My brother and I would ride our bikes there every afternoon."

Zoe wasn't sure what surprised her more: that Jake shared a personal memory or that he had a family. For some reason, she'd assumed he was alone in the world. *Because that's the way he wanted it to be.* Knowing the truth, however, made his isolation even sadder.

"Where's your family now?" she asked.

"My dad's in Florida. I'm not sure where Steven is. New York, I think. We've..." He picked at the sand on the rock. "We've, uh, lost touch."

In other words, he cut ties with them. *Such a shame.*

"No, it's not."

She hadn't realized she'd spoken aloud. However now that the words were out, she saw no reason not to continue. "You don't think your family misses you?"

"My family's better off." The air stilled while he sipped from her coffee cup. Zoe's insides stilled as well. Did he really believe such a thing? That his family wouldn't want him around?

He must have sensed her question. "I'm not the same person they knew before. I don't have anything to offer them. Not anymore."

"You don't know—"

"Yes, I do."

Zoe bit her lip. She disagreed, but arguing would only close him off again, and she didn't want to spoil this tenuous whatever-you-want-to-call-it they'd formed.

Looking down, she realized, guiltily, she still held the starfish in her hand. "Sorry, little guy. Didn't mean to forget about you." *It's just that the man sitting on the rocks tends to make the rest of the world fade away.*

She set the creature back under water, on the rock she found him on. "Wonder what other critters we might find if we looked."

"Dismembered crab claws and smashed clams, most likely."

"You're no fun."

"Never said I was."

Bet he was once. Before the demons took hold. Suddenly, she was possessed by an idea. Frivolous, perhaps, but if she could get him to go for it, well... it might do him some good. "Want to come on a scavenger hunt with me?"

The minute she made the suggestion, Jake chuckled. A low throaty rumble that came from deep within his chest and made her long to hear a full-blown laugh. "You want me to help you look for broken seashells?"

"Don't forget skate cases. Finding the starfish has me feeling nostalgic. Plus, a walk on the beach is exactly what I need to clear my head."

"So take the tube of terror."

"Reynaldo would only try and eat my discoveries, and as good a companion as he is, sometimes it's nice to have a human being around to talk to." *Something you need to realize, too.* "What do you say? Will you keep me company?"

Jake shook his head. "I don't think so, Zoe."

"Bet I can find more sea glass than you."

Again, he gave a chuckle. God, but the sound was musical. "Are you always so persistent?"

"Yes." It was, as Paul used to say, one of her most annoying qualities. Not knowing when to quit. In this case, she probably should. Quit, that is. But she couldn't. Somehow in the last two minutes, her frivolous idea had become a challenge. This was the most open she'd seen Jake since they'd met. She couldn't shake the idea that if he allowed himself to relax, Jake might let down some of those walls he'd built around himself.

And okay, she wanted to keep this whatever-it-was going on a little longer. Given Jake's mercurial moods, who knew how long it might last?

"A half-hour walk. That's all I'm asking. Then I'll leave you alone for the rest of the day."

From the way he shook his head, she was ready for another refusal. It surprised her, therefore, when one didn't come. "One half hour. And then you'll leave me alone?"

Zoe smiled, thrilled with her victory. "Scout's honor."

What the hell was he doing? First, against all reason, he brought Zoe a cup of coffee. No, he didn't simply bring her coffee; he sat and listened to her problems. Now here he was beachcombing, for God's sake. He'd lost his freaking mind.

Actually, he could explain the coffee. From the moment she moved in, Zoe had this annoying sparkle about her, a kind of energy that made her impossible to ignore. When she saw the flowers, that sparkle dimmed. Her features fell and she lost all expression. It reminded him of the reflection he saw in the mirror every morning. Except, on Zoe, the melancholy and flat, mirthless eyes looked all wrong. So, when she threw away the roses and retreated to the beach, he felt compelled to check on her. To make sure the dimness was only temporary. Naushatucket didn't need two empty souls.

All right, maybe he was curious, too. The flower delivery bugged him for some reason. Who the hell sends flowers over on the damn ferry? He knew they were from the ex as soon as she tossed them, and he wanted to know what kind of man could snuff out Zoe's brightness.

Come to think of it, that brightness was to blame for this whole beachcombing craziness, too. Her whole damn face lit up finding that starfish; he was afraid to say no and watch it dim again.

Yeah, he didn't want to disappoint her. That was the reason he agreed.

It certainly wasn't because she looked sexy as hell standing ankle-deep in the tide pool.

Nor was that the reason he was still accompanying her long after the half-hour mark had passed.

The tide had come in. Formations that previously rose ten feet out of the water were now half-submerged, making exploration difficult, but Zoe didn't seem to care. She scrambled up and over the rocks, scouring the sand and tide pools. Her most exciting discovery so far was a sea slug—a sighting that had her wrinkling her nose and uttering a high-pitched "Eww!"

He himself wasn't doing too much searching. He found watching her way more entertaining. How she caught her lower lip between her teeth while she concentrated and how, when she thought she spied something, she would kneel down and bring her face close to the object she wanted to study. He simply walked along behind her, carrying both their shoes. Been a long time since he'd felt cool moist sand under between his toes.

"And once again, I've cornered the market on skate cases." Zoe tossed a four-pronged hollow tube at his feet. Jake laughed.

The sound sent guilt tearing through him. This wasn't right. Him, relaxing. Laughing. Enjoying himself.

Why couldn't he stop?

Meanwhile, Zoe had scrambled her way to the top of yet another rock formation and now appeared stuck. Jake knew why. The rocks on this section of the beach were particularly mossy, and when covered with water, hard to stand on.

"Need a hand?" he asked.

She shook her head. "I think I can make it. If I look where I'm going." Gingerly, she stepped down, her foot finding a moss-covered point.

Jake saw the impending calamity before it happened. The moss, soaked from waves, had become a blanket of slime that, when it met with Zoe's wet foot, became even more slippery. She immediately lost her balance and fell. The momentum propelled her forward, and she wound up half falling, half running down the remaining three rocks. Acting on instinct, Jake moved in to catch her, reaching the base in time for Zoe to land full-force onto him. Together they fell backward in a heap, Jake sprawled in the sand, Zoe sprawled across him.

As soon as they each caught their breath, Zoe said, matter-of-factly, "I slipped."

"No kidding," he replied.

"Did I hurt you?"

He shook his head. "My backside caught the brunt of the impact."

"That's good— Oh, your hip!" She pushed herself up from his chest. "I'm so sorry!"

"Don't be." The pain in his hip was nothing compared to the throbbing that flared elsewhere along his body when she shifted her weight. Heat, primal and instinctive, spread to every part of him. He'd felt every inch of her tiny frame, from her hips pressed against him, to her toes tickling the denim of his jeans.

During the fall, her glasses had fallen off, leaving him with an up-close, unobstructed view of her pale blue eyes. The most polished sea glass in the world couldn't come close to how gorgeous they looked. And her lips. He'd never noticed how plump and full they were.

"You've got sand in your hair," he murmured. Before he realized what he was doing, his hand reached up and combed the strands from her face. The dark locks were warm from the sun. And soft like silk. He twisted the strands between his fingers.

"We should get up before a wave lands on us." Though he said the words, he didn't feel any urgency. What he wanted was an excuse to touch her hair again. Dear God, when was the last time he'd felt something so soft?

Zoe smiled. "Afraid we'll wash out to sea?"

"You might." Taking care not to tip her off, he raised himself up onto his elbows. "I've seen sand fleas bigger than you."

"I'm not sure if I should be flattered or insulted."

"Ever see what a sand flea looks like? Definitely be flattered."

Her skin was already pink from the sun, and the blush covering her cheeks only deepened the color. It reminded him of pink frosting. If he ran a finger on her cheek, would it come away tasting sweet? His mouth watered with curiosity.

What on earth had her ex been thinking? He had to be insane, cheating on someone so beautiful and sweet. And sending flowers to apologize? The man should have come in person to beg on his knees for forgiveness. Kissing those perfectly plump lips 'til they were sighing with desire.

He couldn't help himself; he brushed some imaginary hair from her cheek. The softness under his fingers took his breath away. Her eyes had darkened, their paleness eclipsed by her widening pupils.

He felt pounding against his ribs. Took a moment, but he realized it was Zoe's heart beating in rhythm with his. She probably had no idea he could feel it.

God, but he bet those lips tasted amazing. He bet

every inch of her did. They were so close, too. All he needed to do was lift his head and they'd be his.

"Zoe?" His voice sounded raw and rough to his ears.

She raised her head, edging those lips closer. "Yes?"

It took all his resolve, but he found the right words. "You need to move first."

"I can't." The blush managed to deepen yet another shade. "I don't know where my glasses landed."

Oh, right. Her glasses. He'd been so mesmerized by her blush, he'd crazily mistaken it for arousal. Somewhere deep inside him, the truth brought a sense of relief. What else would it be?

Patting around the sand, he located the frames. She grabbed them from his hand like they were a life raft, and shoved them into place. "Thanks."

Her vision restored, she rolled off, leaving a cold empty sensation in her wake. The feeling was so sudden that his hand automatically began reaching out to pull her back. Fortunately he kept his head.

Or rather Zoe kept it for him. "I'm hungry," she announced.

Her pronouncement pulled him from his inner struggle. "Excuse me?" he asked as he struggled to his feet.

"I haven't had anything to eat since dawn, and I'm starved. Aren't you?"

"Hadn't thought about it." Eating had long ago

become something he did when he needed to do; he didn't give meals—or lack of them—much thought.

"Well, I have. It's late afternoon, in case you haven't noticed."

It was? How the hell did a whole afternoon pass by?

"Poor Reynaldo must be starving, too. He hates it when dinner is late."

"Then you better go feed the both of you."

"Hmm." She was looking at him, the sparkle all of a sudden reappearing in her eyes, brighter than before. Jake got a sinking sensation.

"Or..." She smiled. "I've got a better idea."

Better was a relative term.

"I still can't believe I agreed to this," he said.

"Why not?" Zoe tossed a piece of driftwood onto the campfire, sending sparks shooting into the sky. "I can't cook and you don't have any food. This is the perfect solution."

Jake shook his head. A campfire. His earlier assessment was right—he was out of his freaking mind. Actually, when Zoe first suggested the idea, he told her she was the one out of her mind. If only he hadn't slipped up and mentioned that his refrigerator was empty... She'd argued him into a corner at that point. "I'm going to build the fire anyway so you might as well join me. What else are you going to do? A man's got to eat, right?" She'd badgered him 'til he had to say yes, just to get her to stop.

Go ahead. His mind flashed back to them lying together on the beach. *Tell yourself you don't really want to be here.*

Meanwhile Zoe was busying herself with piercing a hot dog with a skewer. Soon as he acquiesced, she'd dashed across the street for supplies. After ordering him to gather wood, of course. She was, Jake was slowly learning, a bundle of enthusiasm. Once she made up her mind to pursue something, she wouldn't be deterred.

Or ignored, for that matter, he thought with an internal smile.

Hot dog in place, she handed him the skewer. "What I can't believe," she said, "is that you've never cooked over a campfire before."

"I didn't say that. I said I'd never roasted hot dogs over a fire."

"My mistake. What have you cooked?"

He thought of the chipmunks, snakes and other creatures scrounged during survival training. "You don't want to know."

"Something tells me you're right."

Reynaldo came trotting up looking for a snack. The dachshund, who'd returned with her, was happily covered with sand. Zoe reached into her sweatshirt pocket and pulled out a dog biscuit. "Here. This should tide you over." Rey took the treat and settled contentedly on a nearby towel.

"My dad loved campfires on the beach," she said. "We used to have them once a week. Hot dogs and S'mores. Inevitably he'd set the marshmallows on fire. Funny how some memories stick with you, isn't it?"

"Hmm." More than she'd realize.

"Then again, I suppose mine are tainted by childhood nostalgia. I guess that's human nature for you. We tend to romanticize the past. Paint it better than it really was."

Jake didn't answer. *If only all memories worked like that.* But some could never be repainted. They were doomed to repeat themselves with perfect Technicolor accuracy. Zoe didn't need to hear that, though. She, like so many, was better off untouched by dark thoughts.

He looked over at his companion. She was perched on her knees, carefully holding her hot dogs over the flame. You'd think from the way she was turning the skewer—slowly, like a rotisserie—she was cooking a gourmet meal. Her skin was pink from the sun and heat. And her hair was pulled back in a haphazard ponytail. It wasn't hard to picture her as a young girl licking marshmallow from her fingers.

"It's going to burn," she said, jerking him from his thoughts. He realized she was looking at him.

"If you stick your hot dog in the flames like you're doing, you're going to burn it."

Turning to the fire, he saw that he'd absently stuck his skewer deeper into the flame. "I like them burned. The carbon adds flavor," he added when she quirked a brow above her frames.

"Right."

"You don't believe me?"

"What I believe is I've finally found something you're not good at." The way she cocked her head reminded him of Reynaldo, all eyes and cuteness. "Hard to imagine you not being good at everything."

The compliment hit him cold and he looked to the fire. "I'm far from perfect, Zoe."

"I never said you were perfect. Just capable. Extremely capable."

He had no business feeling pride from her compliment, but he did anyway. "I am a handyman."

"Good thing, too, for me," she replied with a grin that made his pride stand at attention. "Otherwise the bats and I would be roommates. However..." She leaned over and, taking his hand, adjusted the angle of his skewer. "That doesn't change the fact that you can't cook over a fire."

Jake's skin tingled where she touched him. He found himself contemplating lowering the skewer again so she'd repeat the action.

"You're in good company, by the way," she told

him. "When my father burned the marshmallows, he claimed the flame added flavor, too."

"See? Great minds think alike."

Jake fell silent. The beach was empty now, the locals having gone home for the evening. Only he, Zoe and the dachshund remained.

He looked at the fire. It felt strange, seeing flames without destruction. But here, watching the sparks rise and fade into the night, it was almost—*almost*—possible to imagine a more innocent time. Before everything turned dark and painful.

It was Zoe, he decided. Her enthusiasm and energy trumped everything around her. Odd, but what he'd first found incredibly annoying, tonight he found amazingly calming.

Looking over, he noticed she was lost in thought, she, too, focusing her attention on the fire. Shadows moved across her face like dancing clouds.

"Would you mind if I asked you a personal question?" she asked.

Jake's spine stiffened.

"Did you ever think that somewhere in life you took a wrong turn?"

Of all the questions she could ask, that wasn't one he expected. *Every damn day,* he wanted to say. "This is about the ex, isn't it?"

"Paul?" She shook her head. "No. Maybe a little. It's just that I can't help but wonder how I ended up where I am in life."

"You mean divorced?"

"My divorce, my career, everything. I mean, I like what I do, but lately..." She lifted her shoulders in a sad shrug as if the gesture alone was enough to fill in her thoughts. "It's like I'm out of step with the universe. Know what I mean? Like the universe is sending me signals and I'm missing the meaning."

"What kind of signals?"

"Beats the hell out of me. Don't fall for a needy golf pro?" She gave another hollow laugh. He hated the sound. It lodged heavily in his gut, like lead. He sought to change the subject, hoping at least one of them could shake the encroaching despair.

"How do you become an advice expert anyway?" he asked. It was something he'd wondered since she'd told him what she did.

"My college newspaper used to have a column and when the writer graduated, I volunteered for the position. I enjoyed it so much that after graduation I decided to see if I could keep it going. I started with a blog, and voilà, 'Ask Zoe' was born. All because I wanted to be useful."

"Useful?" Sounded like an odd word choice.

"Helpful," she corrected, brushing sand from her legs. Not, however, before he caught a flash of something in her eyes. "I like being helpful."

Making her the target for every sad story that came along.

"Anyway, I'm being maudlin." She broke off a

piece of hot dog and tossed it to Reynaldo. "That's the downside of being nostalgic. For every memory, you get a matching what-if."

And for every what-if, you got ten more. Then a hundred. Until eventually you have so many regrets and what-ifs you can hardly breathe from the weight. Jake heaved a sigh. The contentment he'd felt earlier, however slight, vanished, replaced by the familiar weight of guilt.

Did you really think you could escape yourself?

He stared into the flames. At the red-orange tongues. Just like Zoe warned, his hot dog had caught fire. The smell of burning meat met his nostrils. He watched as the flames turned the casing blistered and black.

Like a length of charred flesh.

Bile rising in his throat, he hurled the skewer into the fire. The force sent ashes scattering across the sand. A stray piece of wood flew up and landed on the back of his hand. Jake hissed from the contact.

"What the—?" Zoe was in front of him before he saw her move. "Are you all right? Did you burn yourself? Let me see."

He must have clasped his fist to his chest, because all of a sudden he could feel her soft touch as she pried open his fingers. "Doesn't look too bad," he heard her say. "We should wash off your hand with cold water, though."

Before he could protest, she slipped away. She was

back a moment later, a bottle of water and a paper towel in her hand. "This will have to do for now. When you get home, you can put some antibiotic ointment on."

He tried to shake off her attention. "It's just a burn. I've had worse." Far, far worse.

Although right now, his heart seemed to be slamming against his ribs more violently than it ever had under fire.

"Even a small burn can get infected," she retorted as she pressed the damp cloth to his skin. The lemon scent of her hair rose up to greet his nostrils and he inhaled deeply. More than grounding, it was the scent of clean and home and everything good he'd forgotten could exist. He breathed and breathed until his lungs were so full he feared they might burst. He wanted to lose himself in the aroma, in Zoe herself with her silky sweet skin and promised refuge. An ache, unfamiliar yet strong as steel, took hold in his chest.

Zoe looked up at him from beneath her lashes. "Better?"

Hell no. He was off balance and out of breath. And God, how he ached.

"Yes." It wasn't a complete lie. His hand didn't hurt anymore.

"Good." She smiled. Jake's insides spiraled into free fall. A groan rose in his throat. Just a slip of his arm around her waist. That's all it would take to pull her lemon-scented brightness tight.

Refuge. It called to him. *She* called to him.

Expectancy hung in the hair. Zoe felt it, too. There was no mistaking the desire dancing in her eyes.

He heard a dull thud as the water bottle fell to the ground. Free, her hand reached toward his face, her fingers shaking as they tracked the line of his jaw. Jake's breath caught. The feathery touch stoked the fire inside him. He wanted her. God, but he wanted her.

But then what? Did he kiss her senseless? Lose himself in the sanctuary of her arms for a night, taking what she so willingly offered without giving anything in return? Because what did he have to give but emptiness and darkness and cold?

What kind of man would that make him?

No, he couldn't—wouldn't—do that to her. She'd already been used by one man—he wouldn't add to the list. He might have precious little honor left, but he had enough.

Summoning up all his resolve, he broke away. "I'll take care of myself now," he told her.

For a second, Zoe didn't move except to sway in his direction. Damn if he didn't want to grab her up again. He had to stomp a few feet away to resist the temptation.

"I don't want— I don't need you to play nursemaid." The harshness of his words made him wince. Who was he trying to admonish, her or him?

"I didn't mean to presume otherwise," she replied in a soft voice. So soft it hit him square in the gut. He turned, ready to apologize, only to catch her staring sightlessly into the fire.

Earlier in the day he'd wondered what kind of man could kill her brightness. Now he knew.

How many more people were going to be hurt because of him?

CHAPTER SEVEN

"I CAN'T decide if I like the light grey or the dark."

"Zoe, they're roof shingles, not a work of art."

It was the first time they'd interacted in two days, and Zoe wasn't in a hurry for the conversation to end. Following his abrupt departure the other night, Jake had become a human ghost. He was at work on her roof before she could say hello and packed up before she could say goodbye. He even brought lunch, which he insisted on eating while working.

"I've got other customers to get to," he'd told her when she commented on his workaholism. "Your roof repairs can't take all summer." A perfectly valid reason, if...

If she didn't have the nagging feeling he was avoiding her.

"If I'm going to have this roof for twenty years, then I want to make sure I like what I end up with," she told him, picking up the samples for another look.

Behind the counter, Javier snickered. Jake rolled his eyes and leaned against a nearby shelf.

It wasn't that Jake hadn't been cordial. He'd waved when she had waved, spoken if she'd started a conversation. Once she caught him scratching Reynaldo under the collar. Despite all that, however, something between them was *off*.

She set the samples on the counter. "I'll take the light gray. They go best with the paint."

"You sure? There might be some samples in the back you haven't looked at," she heard Jake mutter.

"Very amusing. I'd like to see you pick something out from a three-inch square."

"I wouldn't have needed that big a sample."

Zoe shot him a smirk. The exchange was the most relaxed conversation they'd had all morning.

For the past two days, she'd felt as if they were both on guard, with each of them monitoring the other's actions. She knew why, too. That little slip of hers while standing at the campfire.

Who wouldn't be freaked out by their neighbor making goo-golly eyes at him? Lord knows what she'd been thinking by touching his cheek.

Check that. She knew exactly what she'd been thinking—or in this case, not thinking. She chalked it up to too much sun and the distracting way the campfire light danced across his features, drawing her in.

And what excuse do you have for the other times? a voice in the back of her head asked.

Javier promised to have the shingles delivered first thing the following morning. While he was writing up the order, Zoe noticed the young man stealing a glance in Jake's direction. He'd been doing so their entire visit.

She turned to give Jake a reassuring smile, pretty sure he'd seen the looks as well. The handyman stood with one hip propped against the shelf and his thumbs hooked in his pockets. To anyone who walked by, he looked like a man casually waiting on his companion. Unless, that is, you were like Zoe and noticed how stiffly he held his shoulders, or that his gaze remained frozen on a spot right behind Javier's left shoulder.

What was going through his mind? Coming back here had to be awkward after his abrupt exit last time. Yet he handled the clerk's surreptitious stares with aplomb. Zoe was impressed.

Then again, Jake continually impressed her. More so than he should, she worried.

She returned her attention to the clerk. "How are you doing?" After all, it had been his bad news that precipitated everything. "I'm sorry about your friend."

"*Obrigado.* I'm doing well. How are you, *senhor*?" he asked Jake. "Are you feeling better?"

The slight rise of color in his cheeks was the only

indication Jake found the question uncomfortable. "Better," he replied. To Zoe, he added, "I'm going to wait outside. Come find me when you're finished."

Behind the counter, Javier looked like a young boy who'd been reprimanded. "I ticked him off, didn't I?"

"Who? Jake?" She shook her head. "Not at all. He's only trying to speed me along."

"Still, I shouldn't have said anything. Ira told me Captain Meyers is touchy about things. I wasn't thinking."

Captain Meyers. She knew he'd been an officer.

She was surprised to hear the manager had shared the information after being so closemouthed with her. Then again, traipsing back and forth between the stores, Javier wasn't exactly an outsider the way she was. Would the young man have the same protective standards as Ira? Hoping to look casual, she twisted her credit card between her fingers. "Did Ira tell you anything else?"

"Only that he was injured in an attack. And that it was bad."

An understatement, to say the least. Zoe turned her gaze toward the front of the store and the tall shadowy figure on the other side of the glass.

"Yes," she replied softly. "I think it might have been very bad indeed."

* * *

Jake was waiting on the sidewalk when she emerged. "Sorry about in there," she said, joining him.

"You have nothing to apologize for."

Perhaps, but she felt like she should. "Javier's worried he ticked you off."

"He'll recover."

"And you?"

"What about me?"

"Well, it had to be awkward being back here. I mean after last time…"

He'd started down the sidewalk, slowly so Zoe could keep up. Now he paused. "That was almost a week ago. I'll recover, too."

Would he? She wasn't so certain. Though his eyes were masked by his sunglasses, she was pretty sure that, if visible, they'd belie his nonchalance. By now she'd learned he wasn't as indifferent as he pretended to be. Though she also knew if she challenged him, he'd deny the charge.

"I was wondering," she said, as they started up the pace again, "do you mind if we stop at the general store before heading back to the marina? I need to buy Reynaldo some dog chews."

"Wouldn't want the tube of terror going without, would we?"

"Trust me, we don't. Besides, I wouldn't mind getting some better coffee beans. The ones at the 'gourmet—'" she framed the word with her fingers "—store in Pitcher's Hole are more gour-maybe and—"

He cut her off. "I don't really have the time...."

There it was again, that *off* feeling.

"Look," she told him, "the shingles won't be delivered until tomorrow and by the time we get back home it's going to be too late to start a project for someone else, since you'd only have to stop and finish my roof. And if I don't run my errands now, I'll have to take the ferry back, and what with it being off-season and the boat not running every day..."

What Zoe didn't mention about the errands was that they were an excuse to spend more time together. Going home meant returning to their cordial stand-offishness, and she wasn't ready to go back to that quite yet. At least here on the island, Jake had to make conversation.

Why that mattered, she wasn't sure, but it did.

"Fine." Jake let out an exasperated sigh, though to Zoe it sounded a tad too loud and a tad too long to be serious. "We'll go run your errands. But—" he held up a finger "—if you dither half as long about coffee as you did about the shingles, I'm leaving you behind. I don't care if the ferry doesn't run again until July."

She reined in her victory smile. "Oh, don't worry. I'm very definitive when it comes to my coffee."

The general store was exactly as the name implied: a catchall tourist destination selling everything from souvenir T-shirts to whole bean coffee and imported cheese, with knickknacks and brassware thrown in. True to her word, Zoe selected her coffee in record time. Likewise, the sunscreen and fresh-baked biscuits. Ironically, it was Jake who ended up slowing their progress. He walked up and down every aisle of the store studying the contents.

"You mean in all the times you've come to this island, you've never been in this store?" Zoe asked him.

"Not once."

How sad. Granted, visiting some tourist shop wasn't a big deal. But she doubted Jake visited any kind of store, unless he absolutely had to. It was as if he did the bare minimum to exist: eat, sleep and work. With eating and sleeping being optional, she'd bet. No friends, no extraordinary experiences, no joy. Not much of a life.

At least he appeared to be enjoying this visit. "Look at this," he said. "All-natural, Himalayan dog chews made from reindeer antlers." He frowned. "Regular antlers aren't good enough?"

"Says the man who just slipped a package of Aunt Millie's Organic Canine Cookies in my basket."

"That's different. I want to see if dogs actually like those things."

"Right. And the fact it's shaped like a chipmunk is a coincidence." She laughed and gave his rib cage a nudge. "Face it, my dog's growing on you."

Jake looked down at her smile and their eyes

locked. Silence, heavy with unspoken thoughts, swept between them. Zoe was suspended in place, as if her moving hinged on what he was about to say. Jake's gaze dropped to her mouth, and a tremor ran down her spine. "Maybe it's not only the—"

"Jake? Jake Meyers, is that you?"

A balding man in his sixties who was wearing a Black Dog Tavern T-shirt approached from the other end of the aisle. "Talk about a fortunate occurrence."

From the look on his face, Jake obviously didn't agree.

"You, Captain Meyers, are a very difficult man to reach. How many messages have I left? Three? Four?"

"The fact I didn't get back to you should have been a hint."

The man let out an indulgent-sounding laugh and rubbed a hand over his scalp. "So, are we going to see you at the ceremony? We'd like to get as many vets on the dais as possible."

"Ceremony? What ceremony?" Zoe's curiosity got the best of her and she spoke up. When the men looked in her direction, she offered a sheepish smile. "Sorry. Didn't mean to interrupt."

"Nonsense. A pretty lady is never an interruption. I'm Kent Mifflin, by the way," he greeted, holding out his left hand. That was when Zoe noticed his right hand had been replaced by a prosthetic hook.

"And the ceremony," he continued, after she'd introduced herself, "is the upcoming Flag Day dedication."

"You all celebrate Flag Day?" The June fourteenth holiday wasn't a largely recognized one, so she was surprised. Come to think of it, however, she had seen red, white and blue fliers in store windows around town.

"Normally, no, but one of our summer residents, Jenkin Carl—ever hear of him?"

"The artist?"

"That's him. He and I served together and I convinced him to make a statue to help honor the veterans from the Cape Cod islands."

"How wonderful." She looked to Jake, who looked away.

"Anyway Jenks can't get here until after Memorial Day, and since Fourth of July is always so crazy, we settled on Flag Day. We were hoping Captain Meyers—"

"Jake." The sound of his interruption startled them. "Just Jake," he repeated.

"Sorry, old habit," Kent said. "We were hoping Jake would join us."

"I can't," Jake replied.

Kent looked about to press, but Jake's expression stopped him. "That's too bad," he said, his voice slow and strangely understanding. The older man regarded him for another second or two, and then he pulled out his wallet. "If you find your schedule opens up, give me a call. I'll make sure they save you two seats at the post-dedication breakfast. It was a pleasure meeting you, Zoe."

"Same here."

Jake remained silent as stone. All the humor from earlier had vanished. His face was distant, his jaw clenched so tightly, she feared the bone might crack from the pressure. "You ready to go?" he asked when Kent was out of view.

Zoe nodded. Not until she reached the checkout did she notice that Kent had dropped his card in her basket. She slipped it into her pocket before Jake noticed.

To her credit, she managed to wait until they'd rung up their purchases and were almost to the dock before circling the conversation around to the encounter in the store. "So, your friend Kent seemed nice."

True to form, Jake looked straight ahead, his expression stony and unemotional. "He's not my friend."

Right, he didn't do friends. How could she have forgotten? "This ceremony he's organizing sounds like a pretty big deal. Too bad you can't attend."

"I have to work."

Again, Jake stared straight ahead as he spoke. A tiny flinch of his jaw muscle betrayed his tension... and told Zoe his answer was nothing more than an excuse. "I'm sure whoever your customer is, he or she would understand if you rescheduled, given the circumstances."

"I don't want to."

"Reschedule or attend?"

Finally he turned to her, and despite the sunglasses, Zoe could feel his glare. "Why do you care?"

Good question. Why did she care? What Jake did or didn't do should be of no matter to her. But it was. Watching him battling himself caused her professional instincts to kick in. She'd grown so used to people asking for advice, she'd begun dispensing guidance unsolicited.

Yes, she thought to herself, that had to be the reason. Habit. Her ingrained need to help. Any other reason would imply she was getting personally involved with Jake, and she wasn't. She wouldn't. She couldn't.

You almost kissed him by the campfire. If that's not getting involved, what is?

Quick as it came, she shoved the memory aside. What mattered right now was Jake.

"Would my caring be so awful?" she asked him.

"Your caring would be a waste of time. What I do—or don't do—is none of your concern."

He must have realized how hard his comment sounded, or perhaps he caught her stunned expression out of the corner of his eye, for his face softened. "I'm sorry, that was uncalled for. I know you mean well. But you're better off spending your energy on the people who want help."

Want. Can't. He threw those two words around a lot. He couldn't do this; he didn't want that. But what about what he *needed?*

Let me in, Jake, she implored silently. *Let me be there for you. Let me...*

She swallowed the first word choice that came to mind, replacing it with a phrase far less risky to her heart. *Let me care what happens to you.*

They cruised back to Naushatucket in silence. For once, Zoe refrained from filling the quiet with conversation. She was far too distracted figuring how to draw out Jake. Unfortunately, no solution came and when they pulled into her driveway, Jake was poised to depart immediately.

Zoe scrambled to think how she might keep him around. "Would you like to try some of the coffee I bought?" she asked. "Guarantee it'll convert you for life."

He shook his head. "No thanks. I'm coffee'd out."

"Then how about a cold drink? You've got to be hot and thirsty after all the walking we did. We could cool off by the tide pool."

"Not today. I've got paperwork I should catch up on."

"You at least have to come in and give Reynaldo the cookie you promised."

"Give him the cookie for me. I'll get those shingles first thing in the morning."

He was pulling away. Literally. The engine revved as he shifted into reverse, preparing to leave.

Zoe planted her hands on the open driver's window. "Jake, wait."

He sighed. "Look, Zoe, I told you, I've got paperwork to do."

Before that it was customers that needed his attention. And before that her roof. All sound reasons that might very well be true, but they were also excuses to avoid talking with her, and they both knew it.

Well, she could use excuses, too. "What about my bat house? You promised to hang it this week."

"Your bat house can wait until morning."

"Not really. Those poor bats have been displaced all week now, and they need a home. It's nesting season. You said so yourself."

Inwardly, she knew calling them the "poor bats" was laying it on a little thick, but she achieved her goal. With an irritated groan, Jake shoved his car back into park.

"Screw the bats. What is it you really want, Zoe?"

Sunglasses or not, his glare could ignite driftwood.

Folding her arms across her chest, Zoe matched his stare. "I want to know why you don't want to attend the ceremony."

There, she'd asked the million-dollar question. Now out, it hung between them waiting for a response.

She got one word. "Because."

"*Because* isn't an answer," she told him. "It's a brush-off. And don't tell me the real reason's none of my business, either," she added, holding up an index finger. "I know it's not my business. I still want to know. Because unfortunately, whether or not you think I'm wasting my time, I want to help you."

"Why?"

Zoe hadn't expected him to turn the tables on her. Nor was she expecting the fluttery ache that struck her chest when he asked. "Because," she began, using his own word against him, "I care."

She watched as the word settled over him, and wished that she could see his eyes. If for no other reason than to see if the yearning emanating from him was real or her imagination.

"I told you, I don't want friends," he said, his face turning toward the steering wheel.

"Too late. The damage is done."

Never had the shake of a head felt so hopeless. "Dammit, Zoe, why can't you leave things alone? You aren't responsible for solving every damn problem in the world. Besides—" his voice grew lower "—some things are so broken they can't be fixed."

He'd said the same thing the other day on the roof.

Dear God, was that how he saw himself? She hadn't realized…

"Nothing is irreparable," she said, echoing her answer from that day. *Not even you.*

"That's where you're wrong."

Slowly, he returned his gaze to hers and from the taut line of his jaw she knew he had to steel himself for what he was about to say. When he spoke, his voice was gruff and raw. "Do you really want to know why the hell I won't attend that ceremony? Because it's a ceremony for heroes, and I'm the last damn person that belongs there."

"You're not making sense." Didn't belong there? "Of course you belong there."

Jake's knuckles were white, he'd gripped the steering wheel so tightly. Zoe wondered if he were trying to snap the metal in two, since he couldn't snap himself. "Forget I said anything."

No. This time she wouldn't let him brush her off when she got close. This time she pushed back.

"What do you mean you don't belong at the ceremony?" And why did he fight so hard against the term hero? "Tell me, Jake. Talk to me. Please."

She watched as Jake turned her words over in his mind, holding her breath for his response. He was waging that internal battle he always battled, debating whether or not to let his barriers down. She hoped this time the results came out in her favor.

Let someone help you, Jake.

"You think it's so simple," he replied aloud, as if he heard her thoughts. "That if I talk, everything will magically fall into place, but you're wrong. I've talked, Zoe." He let out a hollow laugh. "I have talked 'til I'm blue in the face. You know what I learned? Talking doesn't change a damn thing. It doesn't change what happened. And it sure as hell won't bring back the dead," he added in a whisper.

No one should lose a friend. Zoe closed her eyes. She couldn't begin to imagine the horrors Jake had experienced; only a fool would try. But he needn't bear his burden alone, either.

"You're right. Talking won't bring back the dead." Gently, she cupped his cheek, conveying with a touch what her words were unable to say. "But that doesn't change the fact you're here. And that you're very much alive." Or could be, if he'd allow himself.

Jake leaned into her touch and her hopes rose that she'd finally broken through. The promise lasted but a second. No sooner did his shoulders begin to sag than he pulled away again, sitting up straight and pushing away her hand as though her touch burned him.

"That's just it. I shouldn't be here," he rasped, his voice contorted by restrained emotion. "I shouldn't be alive."

CHAPTER EIGHT

JAKE's head hurt. Why the hell did he say anything? Now there'd be no escape. Zoe would press and press until she got the whole story.

Even now, she stood stock-still, waiting for him to explain. God, he missed her touch. So gentle, so comforting. He'd had to pull away. The words wouldn't have come otherwise.

Jake dragged a hand over his face. Funny how words he'd said so many times were still hard to get out.

"We were part of a convoy. The truck in front of us triggered an IED. They must have driven over the trip wire. Next thing I knew, we were taking fire. We never saw it coming."

You should have been on alert, expected the attack. The accusation came as it always did when he made the excuse.

"They had a grenade launcher. We could see the fire coming at us from the hills. I told my driver to blow through, figuring we could outdistance the attack, but then one of the grenades hit the front of our vehicle."

He closed his eyes and the memory played out before him. "It blew a hole right through. I must have... I must have gotten thrown because all of a sudden I woke up on the side of the road and the truck was on fire. My leg... I couldn't drag myself more than a few inches at a time."

The familiar burn started behind his eyelids. Cursing his weakness, he reached under his sunglasses to rub the wetness away.

"Ramirez, the driver—he was trapped. I—I don't know about the others. They were in the truck but..." He took a breath. "I could hear Ramirez screaming. He kept— He kept saying *'Ayúdame. Madre de Dios, ayúdame,'* over and over. I tried. God, I tried, but my leg...

"I couldn't get to them in time. I tried, but I couldn't get to them. The fire..."

Self-reproach rose like bile in his throat, choking him. "Ramirez had just had a baby boy. He'd freaking showed us the photo that morning. Kid was a month old. He never saw him."

"I'm sorry." Zoe's apology floated through the open window, her tender whisper offering absolution. Jake shook it away. He didn't deserve the gift.

"I was their CO. They trusted me to get them home, and I failed." His voice cracked. He tried to swallow, but his throat was too dry. A vice was squeezing the words out of him.

"That's why I won't go to Mifflin's ceremony. How the hell can I sit on the dais and be hailed a hero when I came home and my men didn't?"

He squeezed his eyes, fighting the shudders building inside him, and waited for the chill that told him Zoe had backed away. How could she not, now that she knew what he was, what he'd done?

Then, suddenly, there was a rush of air and he felt himself being enveloped by a cocoon of lemons and salt air.

"Shhh," Zoe was whispering in his ear. "Shhh." Quiet sounds promising peace and salvation. A shudder broke free, tearing through him. With a strangled cry, he collapsed into her, burying his face in the crook of her neck, inhaling that wonderful scent and briefly, ever so briefly allowing himself, for the first time since coming home, to rest.

"Shhh." Zoe couldn't think of anything else to say. She rocked back and forth, her heart crying for the broken man in her arms. His hair felt damp and she realized the moisture was coming from her cheeks.

"It'll be all right," she murmured. "It's going to be all right. I promise."

"No." She felt him shaking his head. "It won't be." Fingers dug into her shoulders as he broke from their embrace. "I can't do this. I don't deserve—"

"Stop." Cutting him off, Zoe pressed her fingers to his lips. "Don't say what I think you're about to say. It's not true."

"How can you say that?"

"Because I know." One look at the anguish in his eyes was enough. "You're a good man, Jake Meyers. A good, decent man."

She moved to touch him again, longing to reestablish the physical connection. To bring him close again.

Awareness flashed in his eyes, and she knew he'd read her thoughts. Seeing his need, the tightness in her chest shifted, changing form until it felt bigger than a simple need to give comfort. Shaking his head, he caught her wrist before she could make contact.

"The man you think I am doesn't exist, Zoe. I'm dead inside."

Zoe's eyes fell to her wrist. To the scarred thumb unconsciously rubbing circles on the inside hollow.

Jake must have followed her gaze because he dropped her hand. "I shouldn't have told you."

"Why? Because I might care?" Too late. That rule had been shattered.

"Because I've got no business getting involved with anyone. Not as a friend, not as a—"

While he was speaking, he'd been leaning in closer. Realizing at the last moment what he was doing, he drew back, closing the door between them instead.

"Not as anything," he said. "I'm sorry, Zoe, but like I told you, some things are too broken to be fixed."

You're wrong. The words died on her tongue. A piece of her broke as she watched Jake pull out of the driveway. The fragment stabbed at her heart, bringing a fresh batch of tears.

"You're wrong," she whispered, out loud this time as he pulled into his driveway and hobbled to the front door. Even though he couldn't hear her, she said the words anyway.

"You're wrong."

"It's called combat trauma, and it's far more common than you think," Kent Mifflin told her.

From behind her coffee cup, Zoe nodded. The two of them were having breakfast in Vineyard Haven. Following his confession, Jake had disappeared into himself. And this time she wasn't imagining the distance. Jake had barely said two words. The shingles arrived, and he buried himself in work. The roof was almost complete. Soon he'd be finished and off on another job. Knowing Jake, that meant she'd see little to nothing of him for as long as he could avoid her. Then she wouldn't see him at all, except at a distance or unless she could make up some kind of house project for him to work on. The idea of never seeing those green eyes again left an ache in the pit of her stomach. So, after another sleepless night where she found herself replaying Jake's story, she called Kent, hoping the understanding she'd heard in the older man's voice meant he knew what Jake was going through.

Her instinct had been correct.

"Problem is," Kent said, "soldiers think they should come home after serving, put the fighting behind them, and go back to regular life. Except it's not that easy. For most of them, the war is still going on. They might not be physically fighting, but they're fighting—" he tapped the side of his head "—in here. Slightest thing can send them back to the battlefield."

Zoe thought of what happened at the hardware store. "Flashbacks."

"They can be hell. For the person experiencing one, it's literally like being right back on the front line. The sounds, the smells, the whole shebang. It's one of the reasons we didn't hold the dedication ceremony on the Fourth of July."

"Because of the fireworks."

"You got it. While most of the crowd's busy oohing and aahing, these men and women are thinking tracer bullets and mortars. Jenkin and I want to honor these people, not make things worse."

Again, Zoe nodded. "When I called, I'd hoped you could give me some insight. I had no idea you were an expert."

"Not an expert—experienced." He brandished the

prosthetic. "Think I simply fell into this good nature of mine? 'Course, back then we didn't have a name for what guys like me were going through. All I knew was I was angry and empty."

Just then the waitress arrived with their orders. While Kent bantered with the waitress regarding the "doneness" of his eggs, Zoe thought about what he'd told her. Angry and empty certainly described Jake. She was certain the incident he'd described the other day, while the worst, was only one of many horrific things he'd witnessed. She'd give anything to erase those images from his head.

"Great gal," Kent said after the waitress left, "but doesn't understand the meaning of 'nonrunny' when it comes to eggs. One of these days I'm going to have to show her myself. Now, where were we?"

"You were telling me about how you learned about combat trauma."

"Oh, right." He bit off a piece of toast. "I was lucky. I had a good support system. My family could afford help. Therapists, rehab, stuff like that. And my grandfather was at Midway, so he had an idea what I was going through. Not everyone's so lucky though. Their families don't know how to help, or they pull away from their families for whatever reason so that they don't have a support system."

Like Jake.

"Can I ask you a question?" Kent asked. She

looked up from her coffee. "Does Jake know you're here talking with me?"

She shook her head. Part of her—a large part—felt enormously guilty for the betrayal. While she hadn't told Kent the exact details of what Jake endured, she'd said enough. Sometimes you have to cross a line when there's no other choice, she rationalized. She only hoped the blow back wouldn't be too harsh.

"Didn't think so," Kent replied.

"I hate going behind his back, but he seems so..." She didn't want to say *broken*, even though that was the best choice, so she shrugged, trying to hide the emotion burning her eyes. "I didn't know what else to do."

"I understand. It's not easy loving someone who's battling demons."

Love? Quickly Zoe held up her palm. "Oh, no, I'm not... I mean, Jake and I aren't..."

Sure, she cared about him. And okay, she was attracted to him. Who wouldn't be? But love? For goodness' sake, she barely knew the man. Besides, even if she were to fall in love again—which she wasn't anywhere near ready to do—people didn't do so in a couple of weeks.

"We're friends, is all," she told Kent. "Jake's my neighbor and handyman."

"Oh." The look on Kent's face made her feel like a kid caught cheating. She had to struggle not to squirm. "My mistake. When I saw the two of you in the store together, I would have sworn…"

He waved off the thought. "Never mind. Either way, he's lucky to have you on his side."

"Except I have no clue what to do to help him."

"You're doing it. Be his friend. Worse thing a guy like him can do is isolate himself. Gives him too much time to think, and believe me, thinking can be your worst enemy. Encourage him to get out and enjoy life."

"Easier said than done," she murmured.

"Hell, if it were easy, the world wouldn't need therapists. Just be patient. There's no overnight fix, I'll tell you that. I'm not sure if there is really a 'fix' at all. The memories never go away. Why do you think I can't stand runny eggs?"

He chuckled, bringing a small smile to Zoe's lips. "Best we can do is learn how to cope," he continued. "A good first step, by the way, would be to get your *friend* to attend the ceremony."

Was it her imagination or did he accentuate the word *friend*?

"Might help to see other vets, too, talk to people who know what he's going through."

"I'll try, but I'm not sure I'll have much luck. He's pretty stubborn, in case you didn't know."

"I know," Kent said with another chuckle. "He and I have crossed paths before. But something tells me if anyone on these islands can convince him, it's you."

"Me?" His confidence in her was astounding. As well as misplaced. "You overestimate my influence. Jake and I have known each other a little over a week."

"And yet he told his story." Kent sawed off a piece of fried egg with his fork and popped it in his mouth. "That's got to count for something."

It didn't surprise her to see Jake on the roof when she drove into her driveway later that day. At the sound of her tires meeting the gravel, he glanced upward, but nothing more. Zoe sighed. Still withdrawn. Her stomach sank when she saw that only a small patch of tar paper remained exposed. Her window of opportunity was closing faster than she thought, taking Jake along with it.

Since the chances of getting Jake to come down and speak with her were slim to none, she had no choice but to approach him. Squaring her shoulders, she marched into the house, grabbed a water bottle and headed back outside.

"Time to mount another rescue mission," she told Reynaldo, who she discovered sleeping on the back step next to a full water dish. "Wish me luck."

Kneeling at the far end of the roof, Jake was hammering away at the shingles with a fury. Drowning his thoughts with work? Or in a rush to be finished?

Because of the unusually hot day, he'd exchanged his T-shirt for a sleeveless tank top. His fully exposed biceps rippled and flexed with each stroke. Their sweaty definition was close to perfection, but it wasn't his physical good looks or his ever-present grace making her breath catch as she stood on top of the ladder. This time it was the lines marring his marbled skin. Lines she now recognized as shrapnel wounds. Her throat caught thinking of the burden being carried by those broad shoulders.

She waited until he'd reached for another nail, then cleared her throat. He turned to look at her straight on, and her heart skipped. Dear Lord, but those eyes... She waved the water bottle. "Hi."

"I'll be done in a couple hours."

"What is that supposed to mean? You'll wait until then for a drink? It's got be close to ninety degrees in the sun. Is it against your rules to have a cold drink?"

"I don't have any rules," he replied. "I'm simply trying to get this job finished."

So he could retreat further. Standing her ground, Zoe waved the bottle again. "Ice cold."

Those must have been the magic words because, giving a long sigh, Jake set down his hammer and made his way to her. While he drained half the bottle in one gulp, Zoe gave thanks to the heat gods and scrambled up the last couple rungs. She perched herself on the peak, making it clear she planned on sticking around.

"I found where the swallow came from," she announced brightly. "Actually Reynaldo did, but I refuse to feed his ego."

"Zoe…"

"He's got a nest on the corner of the shed. Can't believe I didn't notice before. But then…" She took off her glasses and cleaned them on her T-shirt. "Experience has proven I'm slow on the uptake."

"Slow or stubborn?"

"Take your pick." She grinned at him over her shoulder.

Across the street, white caps dotted the dark blue water, the only evidence a breeze existed on this hot day. As she watched the caps turn to waves and foam, Zoe stretched her arms and summoned her resolve. "So…" She swallowed the tremor in her voice. "I was thinking about that Flag Day ceremony."

Behind her, she heard the crackle of plastic, and imagined Jake squeezing the bottle in his fist. Gulping back another tremor, she plunged ahead. "I was thinking maybe you should reconsider attending."

Took less than half a beat for him to respond. "I've got to get back to work."

"Jake—"

"Zoe. I thought I made it clear the other day, there's no way in hell I'm going to that damn ceremony."

"But it might—"

"Might what? Help me find closure? That what you're going to say? Save the argument for one of your columns. I've heard it a thousand times. Standing around admiring some freaking piece of art isn't going to give me closure."

"Neither is shutting yourself off from the world."

"It's worked so far."

"Has it?" She scrambled to her feet, confronting him. "You had a flashback in a hardware store, for goodness' sake. You freaked out at a campfire. How may more times does that have to happen before you admit the truth?"

"I don't have to admit anything."

No, he'd much rather the emotions stayed tamped down so they could eat him alive. "You can only keep things bottled inside for so long before they explode."

Up to that point, Jake had remained stock-still, plastic bottle cracking in his fist as he stared at a point beyond her shoulder. Now he tossed the bottle over the edge and turned back to his work area.

Zoe's frustration boiled over. "You can't keep walking away from this," she snapped at him. "Sooner or later you're going to have to deal with what you're feeling."

"I have work to do, Zoe. I don't have time for this discussion."

"And when your work is finished? What then?"

Stepping toward him, she let her hand come to rest on his shoulder. The muscles beneath were tensed to the point of shaking. Concern twisted in the pit of her stomach. He couldn't keep fighting his own feelings.

"Why won't you let me help you, Jake?" she asked his back.

"I'm not some animal you can rescue, Zoe."

"No, you're a flesh-and-blood man who's been through way more than I can ever imagine."

The breath he let out sounded somewhere between anger and disgust. "I never should have told you."

"But you did, and if you expect me to take a page from your book and pretend it never happened, you're wrong. I can't sit on the sidelines knowing you're in pain. I can't. I care about you too much."

"Well, don't!" The cry echoed through the ocean air. Whirling around, he grabbed her by the shoulders with such ferocity Zoe gasped. His fingers dug into her flesh, holding her in place. Her own hands splayed against his broad chest. Beneath the cotton she could feel his heart racing, certain her own beat as violently.

"Don't," he repeated. His eyes glittered hard and brilliant.

Beneath the hardness, however, she saw his conflict. She saw caution and fear and, dare she say— longing? In that moment, her desperation to help him grew tenfold.

"You think you have to shoulder this burden your-self and you're wrong. You're not alone, Jake. You're not."

Taking a chance, she cupped his cheek, letting him feel the compassion she offered.

His eyes clouded and the grip on her arms soft-ened. "Why can't you leave me alone?"

His protest lacked conviction. "Because that's not my nature."

"Don't you mean you're a sucker for sob stories?"

"Yes, I am." But this time… This time didn't feel like her usual reaction. This time her insides swirled with a host of sensations that went far beyond sym-pathy. Hot, frantic sensations as if she were the one needing him and not the other way around.

Jake's breathing grew harsher. Or was that hers? When they were close like this it was hard to tell. If only she could prove to him how much she cared.

"You're not alone," she whispered again.

"Zoe."

His resolve was breaking. She could tell by the crack in his voice. She ran the back of her hand across his stubble.

"There are so many people out there who want to help you. Me. Kent—"

"Kent?" Big mistake. Jake shoved her aside. "You told Kent?" He looked her up and down, apparently noticing for the first time she'd scaled the ladder in a golf skirt and sleeveless blouse. "That's where you were this morning, isn't it?"

Crap. She knew going behind his back was a bad idea. "We had breakfast and you know what?" She rushed to fill the air before Jake could shut her out. "He had a lot of good information. He understands what you're going through. He's been there. If you would just talk to him—"

"You had no right," Jake spat at her. "No right at all."

"Maybe not, but someone had to start talking. I—"

"Get away." She tried reaching for him and he put his hands up, blocking her path. Erecting his barriers. "I knew it was a mistake to tell you anything. What happened over there is between me and my men."

"Your men are dead!"

She couldn't help herself. His words had kicked her in the stomach and she wanted to lash out. From the way he stumbled back, she couldn't have hit him harder if she physically struck him.

"Don't you think I know that?" he growled. "Not a day goes by that I don't regret the fact I'm here and they aren't."

"Really? Because it looks to me like you're trying to bury them all over again, only this time you're trying to forget they ever existed in the first place!"

Jake's shoulders flinched, and his eyes flashed so

that she feared she'd finally pushed too far. But with all his other feelings, the outburst she expected never came.

"I'll be done with your roof in a couple hours," he said. His voice was flat and controlled. "After that, I think you should look for another handyman. I'm sure your friend Javier can recommend someone."

Inside, a piece of Zoe crumpled. The barriers had slammed firmly in place, thicker than they'd ever been. She felt helpless, useless. Worst of all, she felt...alone. More alone than when she arrived on the island.

Anger welled up inside her. This was what she got for getting involved.

Jake heard the screams. *"Ayúdame! Ayúdame!"*

Flames surrounded him. Hot stickiness covered his legs. When had the ground turned red? He dragged himself forward, toward the truck. His body wouldn't move.

Why couldn't he move? Ignoring the pain, he dragged himself onward. Yet every time he looked up he was in the same damn place.

"Ayúdame!" Ramirez's cries rose above the gun-fire. "Don't forget me!"

"Hang tight, Ramirez! I'm trying."

"Don't leave me, Captain!"

"I won't." But as he looked up, the truck was farther away than before. The fire rose, ready to engulf the vehicle. Inside, his men were screaming.

"Captain! Don't forget us, Captain!"

Breath tearing from his lungs, Jake sat up. What the hell?

He peeled off his sweat-soaked shirt and stumbled to the window. Next door, Zoe's bedroom light shone, its soft yellow glow the only brightness on the moonless night. A yearning—fierce and overwhelming—rose up inside him, forcing him to squeeze the windowsill.

No, he scolded himself. *You can't go there.*

Don't leave me. Ramirez's disembodied voice rang in his ears. *Don't forget us.* The helplessness and self-hatred he always felt following a dream engulfed him. God, but he wished things could be different. If he'd been a minute sooner, moved a foot faster, he might not have this emptiness. Instead of standing alone with his nightmares, he could be seeking solace in a pair of warm arms. A pair of lemon-scented arms.

But things weren't different, were they?

His pain pills were by the bed. Ramirez's cries still in his head, he stumbled to the night stand. As he reached for the bottle, his fingers brushed the photo propped against the lamp. There was no need to turn on the light for him to see it. Like so many others, the image was burned into his memory. Sergeant Bullard—Bulldog—had taken the shot with his cell phone a few days before. To remember their ugly faces, he said. Bullard had been lucky. He'd shipped home that afternoon. Some place in Arkansas.

Don't forget us. Like he ever could.

Ramirez's voice morphed into another. A soft gentle voice that promised comfort and light. "Don't bury them, too," the voice said. He wasn't.

Or was he? Was that what he was doing? Was he burying his men's memory?

He washed his hand across his face. "Dammit, guys," he whispered to the photo. "I'm so sorry."

CHAPTER NINE

"Ow, ow, ow! Crap!"

It was the second time Zoe had sworn in fifteen minutes. Her project wasn't going well.

Jake did his best to ignore her. Whatever she was doing, she could handle it herself. He focused on the account books in front of him.

"Arrrgh!"

Jake threw his pen down. Yesterday's nightmare, a repeat of the nightmare he'd been having for the past three days, had given him a headache, making concentrating difficult enough. The last thing he needed was the racket next door.

"Son of a—"

Oh, for crying out loud! Jake combed through his hair. Time was he could sit in the backyard and balance his receivables undisturbed. Then again, time was his backyard was quiet. B.Z. *Before Zoe.*

What on earth was she doing over there anyway? And since when did he start measuring his life in terms of Zoe's arrival? For that matter, since when did he start measuring his life, period? He was a day-to-day existence guy. And yet...

His eyes drifted toward the fence. A flash of orange caught his eye, causing his chest to constrict. He hated the sensation. For days now, the same damn feeling kept creeping up on him, catching him off guard. Bad enough he had Ramirez haunting him every night. He didn't need to spend his days riding some kind of emotional tidal wave where one minute he was fine, the next he couldn't catch his breath. The fact he'd been having these "incidents" since that night on the beach meant nothing. Nor did the fact that their frequency had increased since he'd finished Zoe's roof.

"Give me a break!"

The sound of a falling ladder crashed into his thoughts. Jake sighed. He was never going to get these books done.

He found her standing beneath the pine tree in her backyard wearing her bright orange T-shirt and a pair of blue gym shorts. Pine needles littered her hair.

"What the hell are you doing?" he asked, ignoring the way his heart lurched at the sight.

"I'm trying to hang the bat house," Zoe grumbled.

Of course. Ever the problem solver, wasn't she?

"Is it necessary to kill your ladder in the process?" Not to mention trampling all over his psyche.

"Stupid thing fell over when I was positioning the bat house."

Jake surveyed the ground. No wonder. Exposed roots burst through the grass-barren area.

Grabbing the ladder, he walked it outward to a flatter section of the ground. "Give me the bat house," he said, putting a foot on the bottom rung.

She refused. "I can hang the damn thing myself."

"Obviously not, based on the racket you're making. Now give me the house so I can get back to my work."

He waited while she contemplated his request. Finally she must have decided pride was less important than getting the job done, and she shoved the wooden box in his direction.

"Here," she muttered, refusing to look at him.

He should be glad she didn't. Her eyes would only churn up his already jumbled insides. But as he made his way to a spot fifteen feet up the trunk, he couldn't help feeling their absence.

He still felt the loss when he finished. Or maybe it was the chill in her voice that left him cold.

"Thanks," she said when he stepped off the ladder. "You can add the charge to my invoice."

"Zoe—"

In the process of walking away, she stopped. He'd been better off when she wasn't looking at him, Jake realized. There wasn't a speck of brightness in her eyes. *You did that,* he reminded himself.

Zoe folded her arms across her chest. "What?"

"I—" What indeed? Was he going to tell her he forgave her for speaking with Kent? Even if he did, saying so would only make her think they had some sort of relationship again. Which they didn't. Couldn't.

This was what he wanted. Distance. Lack of attachment. Best to leave things the way they were.

"No charge for the bat house," he told her.

The heavy feeling in his gut was not caused by the flash of disappointment he caught in her eyes. Nor was the emptiness in his chest because she walked away without a word.

This, he reminded himself, was what he wanted.

Dear Zoe,
I've screwed up. I think I might have fallen for my best friend's boyfriend. I wasn't planning to. It just happened. Now I can't stop thinking about him. What should I do?
In Love and Regretting It

Dear In Love,
First, are you sure you're in love? Because sometimes we convince ourselves of feelings that aren't real, simply because the person says they need you or they make your heart

race every time you see them. Second, nothing good ever comes from loving the wrong person. Trust me. Walk away while you still have the chance.

Zoe

Tossing her glasses on the kitchen table, she rubbed her eyes. Beneath her feet, a low whine could be heard. "Don't start, Rey. You know perfectly well I'm right."

A knock on the front door interrupted their conversation. Instantly, Reynaldo emitted a low growl. Zoe frowned. "What's with you this morning? You mad because Jake didn't stick around and scratch your ears? Get over it." Whatever "it" she and Jake had had going on was over. If "it" had ever begun in the first place. The sooner Reynaldo accepted the fact, the better.

The knock sounded again. A little louder this time. Whoever the person was, he or she had a heavy hand on the brass door knocker. "Come on, Rey, we better see who it is before they bang a hole in the wood."

Undoing the bolt, she opened it a crack and peered out. A perfect tan and a set of perfect teeth smiled down at her.

"Hey, babe."

CHAPTER TEN

UNBELIEVABLE. Her ex-husband sitting in her kitchen drinking coffee was the last thing she expected this morning.

Paul looked good; she'd give him that. Being outside three hundred days a year had given him a permanent golden tan, which his highlighted hair and pale blue golf shirt accentuated perfectly. In fact, everything about him was flawless, from his wardrobe to his features. There wasn't a mark or weathered line on him.

It made him look quite superficial, she realized.

"This is good," he was saying. "You always did have a knack for brewing a fine cup of coffee."

"Seeing how you spent more time in hotels than our apartment, I'm surprised you noticed."

He chuckled. "I've missed that sarcasm, too."

"Yes, it's always been one of my charms." She walked around him to lean against the kitchen counter. "Why are you here?"

"Did you get my flowers?"

"I got them." Memories of Jake bringing her coffee on the beach came to mind, bringing with them an ache in her chest. "You shouldn't have gone to so much expense."

Paul waved off the remark. "Nonsense. You're worth every penny. And I remembered how much you liked calla lilies," he added with a smile.

Actually she liked tiger lilies, but why argue the point? "You still haven't said why you're here."

"To see you, of course. Why else would I come to this godforsaken island?"

Zoe could think of a few reasons, most of them with dollar signs. "I told you on the phone I didn't want to see you."

"That was almost three weeks ago, Zo. You were still angry. I figured you had time to cool down since then."

Had it really been that long? She glanced at the calendar. Dear Lord, it had. She'd been too caught up with Jake to notice time passing. Automatically, her eyes went to the kitchen window, seeking a glimpse of the house next door. How would time pass now? she wondered.

Still at the table, Paul set down his coffee. "I'm assuming you have. Cooled down, that is."

Outside on his run, Reynaldo was barking, angry he'd been banished to the backyard at Paul's arrival. "If you mean do I still want to castrate you for cheating on me, the answer's no. It's not worth the anger."

His sigh of relief filled the room. "Good. I'm glad. I knew you'd realize what we had was too good to throw away, though I admit..."

She heard the sound of a chair, and suddenly Paul was behind her, hands on her hips. "I was willing to get down on my knees and beg if I had to. Still could, if you want." Perfect teeth nipped at her ear lobe.

"Oh, good Lord, stop." She pushed him away. "All I said was I wasn't angry anymore. What on earth makes you think we're getting back together?"

"But, babe, if you're not angry, what's holding you back?"

"How about the fact I don't want you?"

The expression on Paul's face made it seem like she'd spoken a foreign language. "Of course you want me," he said. "We're Team Brodsky. Don't you remember all our plans? Our dreams?"

"Yeah, I remember."

"Then how can you throw all that away? I came all the way here to get you. Surely that means something."

"It means your short game's gone to pot," she told him. "You gave it your best shot, Paul, but Team Brodsky's history. You'll have to find another way to fund your dreams."

"No, I don't believe you." He closed the distance between them. Grasping her shoulders, he forced her close. "I need you, babe," he whispered in his honeyed voice. "I need you too much."

Zoe looked into the brown eyes she'd once found so irresistible. They were really quite bland, she realized. Passionless even as he declared his desire for her. Dear Lord, Jake showed more emotion closed off than Paul did at his most effusive.

Jake. Just thinking his name made her heart catch. She thought of the hunger he tried to disguise when they were close. Of the way she could see down to his soul when she stared into their green depths. Those were the eyes she wanted to look into. Not these.

"You don't need me, Paul. You're just needy."

She moved to push him away, but Paul held fast. His voice grew a little rougher. "I'm not giving up that easily, babe. You're still upset—I get that. Soon as I show you how I need you, though, things will be different."

"No, Paul."

"Remember that time in the condo? You were making toast, and I came up behind you? You said you liked when I took charge." One hand snaked its way to her neck, cupping her jaw, forcing her face upward. His eyes glittered with determination. "That what you want now, babe? For me to take charge?"

Zoe couldn't breathe. Couldn't hear. Blood pounded in her eardrums, drowning everything but her fear. Paul had always been selfish, but he'd never been violent.

Then again, she'd never turned him down before, and he hated to lose.

"Let me go!" She shoved at his shoulders, but years of swinging a golf club left him with a powerful grip. His knee slipped between her thighs. She felt the edge of the counter cutting into her back as he bent her backward.

"I believe the lady said stop."

Jake.

Zoe had never been so relieved to see a man in all her life. Everything would be okay, now. Jake was here.

Crossing the room in one giant step, he grabbed Paul by the collar and yanked the golf pro off her.

"Hey!" Paul hollered, breaking free of his grip. "Who the hell are you?"

"I'm her handyman."

No, thought Zoe, heart in her throat. *He was her hero.*

"Well, if you'll excuse me, Mr. Handyman, my wife and I were having a private discussion."

"Doesn't look like much of a conversation," Jake replied. "And last I checked, Zoe was divorced."

Jake leveled his green eyes like lasers straight at Paul, making it clear he was about to mount another attack. From the way his fingers flexed, she could tell this time he wouldn't be as gentle. Paul folded his arms. Zoe recognized the stance. He wasn't going quietly. That had been his problem as a golfer, too. He never could read the breaks in a green.

"And last time *I* checked," he said with more than a little bravado, "the *handyman* didn't call the shots in my house."

"*My* house." Both men looked at her as Zoe finally found her voice. "This is my house."

Paul nodded. "Sure, babe. Then tell this *handyman* to leave us alone so we can talk." His eyes raked her up and down, as if to silently add, "You know you want to."

The leer made her sick inside. Instinctively she moved toward the one thing that made her feel safe. Jake. "The only person leaving, Paul, is you," she said. "Get out."

Her ex-husband looked like he'd missed a two-inch putt. "You can't mean that."

"You heard the lady," Jake added. "Get out."

"And stay out," Zoe added. "I don't want anything to do with you."

At first Paul didn't budge, preferring to stare at the two of them, and making Zoe fear the altercation would escalate. Venom shone in his eyes. At last, she thought to herself. He's finally showing his true colors.

"You'll be hearing from my lawyers about this, Zoe," he said at last. "I won't stand for being assaulted."

"Neither will I," she replied. "I suggest you rethink that call."

Before he could say anything else, Jake escorted him to the front door, remaining in the open entrance until the golfer had climbed into his car and driven away. As soon as his car disappeared over the horizon, Zoe sagged against the wall. Shivers racked her body. What if...? She hugged her midsection, trying to hold herself together. Jake's large frame appeared before her. "Zoe?"

"What if...? He..." She took a sharp breath. Her lungs burned for the effort. "If you hadn't come by when...you...did..."

The smell of bay rum wrapped itself around her, along with a pair of strong, warm arms. Zoe buried herself in the embrace, letting the security of Jake's presence calm the storm inside her.

"It's okay," she heard him murmur. "Everything's going to be okay."

Zoe believed him. Inside, her heart opened, finally acknowledging the emotion she'd been dancing around for weeks. Everything would be all right. Jake was here.

Her fingers brushed the lip of Jake's breast pocket. Beneath them, she could feel his heart, the erratic beat mirroring her own.

"Zoe..." Jake's voice had deepened. Looking to his face, she saw his eyes had darkened, too, the pupils blown so wide, their green depths were nearly black.

"Do you have any idea how beautiful you are?" he whispered. "So bright. So sweet." His hand reached up and thumbed her cheek. "So tempting."

Her, tempting? She'd have looked away in embarrassment, but he had too tight a hold on her.

Meanwhile, Jake closed his eyes and took a deep breath. Her throat ran dry in anticipation. "You make me feel—" He shook his head. "Doesn't matter."

Yes, it did. "Why not?"

"Because." His smile was sad. "Nothing's changed, Zoe. I'm still as dead inside as I ever was. I could never give back to you what you deserve."

Nothing's changed. Red flashed in front of Zoe's eyes. "Damn you!" The events of the day had left her insides ragged. Hearing his rejection, the tenuous hold on her nerves snapped and she began beating her fists against his chest. "You son of a bitch. Who the hell gave you permission to walk out on life? Huh? Who decided you get to sit on the sidelines while the rest of us carry on?"

"Look, I know you—"

"No, you don't know anything." Hot, angry tears sprang to her eyes. She was sick of it. Sick of caring and not being cared for back. Sick of investing her heart and soul only to get hurt time and time again.

Stay out of the way, Zoe. Don't be a bother, Zoe.
Help me, Zoe.

"Know what?" she asked, wiping her nose.
"Paul might have used me, but at least he wasn't a
coward."

Jake drew in a breath. "A what?"

"You heard me, a coward. At least he went after
what he wanted. He didn't lock himself away, afraid
to live life."

The ragged sound of his breathing told Zoe she
was treading on thin ice, and she didn't care. It was
worth the risk if she could get through to Jake. All
this time everyone had been treating him with kid
gloves, afraid of opening his wounds or making him
lose control. Well, maybe it was time to take off the
gloves and give him a strong dose of truth. Maybe
losing control was exactly what he needed.

"You say you're barricading yourself from the rest
of the world because you're dead inside. You're not
dead. You're afraid. You're afraid to be happy. At
least be that honest. Don't act all noble and pretend
you're doing the 'right thing' when the truth is you're
simply too scared to live."

"Don't." One word. One simple word of warning.
Zoe ignored it.

"Worst thing of all is, you're too blind with guilt
to see happiness when it's standing right in front of
you, offering itself on a silver platter. Tell me, Jake.
How long are you going to keep punishing yourself

for coming home alive? What would your men say if they knew you were using them as an excuse to avoid the world?"

Jake slammed the front door behind him, leaving her standing alone in the foyer. Anger still coursing through her, Zoe watched until his blond head disappeared behind the fence, then buried her face in her hands. She didn't know whether to cry or throw something. Stupid blind fool.

The only bigger fool was her. Because now she knew Kent Mifflin was right.

She was in love with Jake.

Of all the insane ideas…

He was not afraid of living. He *wasn't*. He dragged his sorry self out of bed every morning, didn't he? If anything, he spent every freaking day painfully aware that he was alive.

Zoe was simply wrong. All the more reason he needed to back away from her. Despite all his explaining, she didn't understand he couldn't be the kind of man she deserved. Eventually she'd see the wisdom of his decision and thank him. She would.

Back in his house, he was halfway through grabbing a beer from the refrigerator, when he caught the date on the calendar. June thirteenth. The day before Flag Day. Terrific. Now he had two subjects to ruminate about when the nightmares woke him up. Zoe and Kent Mifflin's big "hero" celebration.

He grabbed a backup beer. Looked like it would be a long night.

The dream was the same as always. Flames surrounding him. The smell of blood and sulfur in his nostrils. Ramirez and the others crying out for him. *Ayúdame! Don't forget us! Ayúdame!*

Jake lay prone in the sand, his body sticky with blood. He was trying to crawl his way to the truck.

Ayúdame! Ayúdame!

A new voice joined the chorus. Soft and sweet, like a siren song. "Over here, Jake! Over here!"

Looking to the hills behind him, he saw Zoe hopping from rock to rock. She wore her orange T-shirt and denim cutoff shorts. Her messy ponytail bounced with each hop she took.

"Get down!" he hollered. "Take cover!"

But Zoe ignored him. "I'm not in danger," she told him. "It's perfectly safe here. Come and see."

He tried. Digging into the sand with his elbows, he pushed himself forward. But he went nowhere.

"Ayúdame!" Ramirez and the others chanted. "Captain! Captain!"

"Jake, come over here. It's safe here!"

"Don't forget us...."

"You'll be safe here."

Back and forth the two sides called to him. Jake

could hear them, but he couldn't move. Not in either direction. The sand had turned into a giant block of cement. He was stuck.

"Move, Jake. Move!" the voices began chanting.

"I can't," he told them. "I can't move."

"You have to move..."

Jake's eyes flew open. His clothes were cold and damp from sweat, but at least he could move his legs again. *He could move.* The realization hit him square in the gut. He. Could. Move.

Swinging his feet to the floor, he moved to stand, but not before glancing at the alarm clock to see how long he'd managed to sleep. Four-thirty, the display read.

Flag Day.

In the end, Zoe went to the celebration because someone should. She'd go and she'd pay tribute to the men Jake lost. Maybe doing so would help her say goodbye to her neighbor.

Nothing else had.

"May I have your attention please?"

Kent Mifflin's voice loomed over the loudspeaker, louder than the waves crashing the beach behind them.

"In 1916, President Woodrow Wilson declared June fourteenth as Flag Day, a day to honor the American flag and the ideals it represented. Therefore, we thought it only fitting that on this day, we honor those men and women who fought under that flag…"

As the speech went on, Zoe let her gaze flit over the crowd. Kent and his committee had to be proud. The turnout was outstanding. In addition to the VIPs and veterans joining Kent on the podium, a sizeable crowd had gathered in the park to watch the ceremony. Some were even in uniform, including several men old enough to be her grandfather. One particular gentleman, with a cane and wearing a brown infantry uniform, caught her eye and winked. She smiled in return.

Yes, sir, Kent managed to draw quite a crowd. Too bad not everyone he'd invited was in attendance.

Even though she knew Jake wouldn't be here, she hadn't expected his absence to feel so glaring.

"…men and women who wore their uniforms so others would not have to…"

She tried telling herself the empty feeling in her chest was guilt for telling him off yesterday, but her heart knew better. The emptiness was Jake himself. He belonged here, with those men and women on the platform.

With her.

"…who suffered and made sacrifices many cannot imagine…"

The sun broke through the clouds, heating the late morning air. Zoe slipped off the cardigan that covered her denim sundress. After three weeks, she'd finally smartened up about New England weather and worn layers. Now if she could only smarten up about other things. Like the fact she'd fallen in love with yet another man who didn't love her back.

She supposed she should be grateful Jake wasn't after her money, too. Though it would be easier if he were. But no, he was trying to protect her from being used and hurt. And hurting her ten times more in the process.

Boy, she sure could pick them, couldn't she? An ex-husband who needed everything, and a man so mired in guilt he was afraid to need anything.

Nothing good ever comes from loving the wrong man. Talk about not following her own advice.

"Therefore, we stand today in their—"

Kent's voice stuttered, catching her attention. Looking up, she saw the older man look to the crowd before continuing, "We stand today in their honor..."

She wasn't sure why—maybe it was his expression that compelled her—but Zoe suddenly turned to her right. A flash of blue toward the rear of the crowd caught her eye.

Dear Lord...

He stood at attention, resplendent in a navy blue uniform. Hair neatly trimmed, the black brim of his cap straight over his eyes. Blue-and-gold epaulets gleamed on his broad shoulders. A rainbow of ribbons hung over his heart.

Dear Lord but he was awe-inspiring in that uniform. It was as if all the confidence and command he carried inside himself had turned outward for the world to see.

Zoe's heart lurched. What made him change his mind about attending?

Sensing her, Jake turned in her direction. Quickly, Zoe looked away. Not before, however, she felt his hard stare. It reminded her of the day they'd met. When he'd wanted nothing to do with her.

On stage, Kent and Jenkin Carl prepared to unveil the statue. Jenkin was explaining something about vision and experience. Zoe didn't listen. Her attention was on the man across the crowd. Glancing back again, she saw Jake had returned his attention to the dais. He knew she was here, and yet he didn't move to join her. It looked like his change of heart was only regarding the ceremony. Tears sprang to her eyes.

"Ladies and gentlemen," Kent announced proudly. "We give you *Sacrifice!*"

The crowd broke into applause. Swallowing back her own emotions, Zoe joined them. Next to her, the old man in uniform snapped into a salute. She pictured Jake doing the same.

Oh, Jake.

As the ceremony drew to a close and the crowds thinned, Zoe saw Jake hanging back. Occasionally someone would walk over to him and say something. He would nod and shake their hand. A couple even saluted. Though the brim of his hat cast his face in shadow, Zoe could tell from his reaction that he was taken aback by the show of respect.

At least he was trying. Maybe she'd helped him a little after all. Too bad she had to break her heart in the process.

"I know you'd convince him," a voice said from behind her.

Kent's face was flushed with enthusiasm. "I couldn't believe my eyes when I saw Jake in the crowd. Your boy looks pretty damn impressive, doesn't he?"

He's not mine. Zoe forced a smile. "I didn't have anything to do with it. I didn't know he was coming, either."

"Once again, I think you sell yourself short."

Not likely. At least not this time. She stole a glance at the other side of the green. Jake stood thirty feet away, but it might as well have been a canyon.

"I'm going to head over and speak with him," Kent said. "You coming?"

Zoe shook her head. She was pretty sure she was the last person Jake wanted to see right now. "I think I'll take a closer look at that statue of yours, if you don't mind."

"Suit yourself. I'll catch you later at the breakfast." He gave her an indulgent pat on the shoulder. "Thanks for coming."

"Thank you," she replied, "for doing a really great thing."

Jenkin Carl's "statue" was really a mass of twisted metal. Black and harshly contrary to its setting, the work featured a trio of spires rising skyward from out of the tangle, as if rising above the chaos. Looking at the piece, Zoe's own insides twisted, too. You could feel the darkness reach inside and touch you.

She ran a hand along the gleaming black surface, thinking of what the statue represented. What men and women like Jake gave up.

Jake. Her insides crumpled. How was she going to spend the rest of the summer with him next door? She'd come to Naushatucket to fix a broken heart, only to find out what a real broken heart felt like.

Guess there was no reason to stay, was there? She sure as hell couldn't heal here now. At least Caroline would be happy.

"Looks like burnt-out wreckage," a familiar voice said.

Her pulse skipped. "I imagine that's what Carl wanted." She forced her voice to stay steady. An emotional scene wouldn't help anyone. "He's trying to evoke an image."

"There are a few images I could do without."

"I imagine so." She kept her eyes on the statue. "I was surprised to see you."

"I'm surprised to see me here, too. But as someone

I know pointed out, we need to remember the ones who didn't come back."

Zoe's vision blurred. She *had* helped. The notion gave her some solace. "I'm sure your men would have appreciated the gesture."

"I'd like to think so."

She could feel his eyes on her now, As always, when he looked in her direction, her skin came alive. This time, Zoe cursed the reaction. Yes, she thought. She had to leave Naushatucket.

"Did you want something?" she asked him.

"I've never seen you dressed up before. You look nice."

"What?" She looked at him to see his eyes had a sheen to them unlike ever before. A light in their depths that turned the green warm and open. Zoe didn't dare believe the expression meant anything. Because if it wasn't true…

She turned back to the statue. "Thank you. So do you."

"You mean this old thing?" It was a lame attempt at humor. Neither of them laughed.

She heard him clear his throat. "Look, Zoe, about yesterday. The things you said were pretty harsh."

Here it was. The part where he told her not to read too much into his change of heart. Zoe was glad she hadn't got her hopes up.

"I spoke my mind," she told him. "I'm sorry

if I was harsh, but I'm not sorry for the words themselves."

"You shouldn't be. You were right." His hand settled on the statue next to hers. "I have been hiding. I've been stuck in my anger and guilt, beating myself up for being alive. I probably would have stayed that way too if you hadn't given me a good harsh dose of reality."

Zoe didn't know what to say.

"It woke me up. Well, a lot of things woke me up. But in the end, I realized there was always one common thread. You. You burst into my world and you wouldn't give up. And you made me long for things I didn't believe I could have."

"And what do you believe now?"

"I don't know. Not fully anyway. But I know I have to start living life again. I need to for my men and I need to for myself."

He slid his hand closer, his little finger grazing hers. Zoe didn't want the hope that rose inside her, but it rose anyway.

"I still have a lot of demons to battle," he said. "And I can't promise I'll get all the way back. Hell, I'm not sure if I'm ready for this at all. But…" His voice caught. "If I'm going to try, I'd like to try with you."

The love in her heart grew a little stronger. She slipped her hand over his, thinking he was the bravest man she knew. "I'd like that, too."

Smiling, Jake raised their hands to his lips. "Good."

A tear dripped down Zoe's cheek. She reached to brush it away, but he beat her to it, his touch reverent and gentle. "I promise I'll do my best not to hurt you."

"I know," she told him. "Just be honest and the rest will fall into place." She touched his cheek. Her fingers grazed his scars, but she couldn't feel them. All she could feel was the warmth. Jake had taken the hardest step today. Looking into his eyes, shining and ripe with sincerity, she had faith he could win. Best of all, this time there wouldn't be some mythical "team" she'd created. It would be a partnership. A real, true partnership. She could feel it in her heart.

"Tell me, Captain," she said, rising on tiptoes, "this 'trying' of yours. It wouldn't involve starting with a kiss, would it?"

The corners of Jake's mouth lifted skyward. "Yeah, I think it can." With that, he leaned forward and pressed his lips to hers.

As kisses went, it wasn't deep or passionate. More like a feathery promise. But the promise was one of love and sincerity. And to Zoe, no kiss had ever been so perfect.

One year later

Jake woke to the smell of lemons and crackling firewood. His eyes scanned the room, searching for the woman who, only an hour before, had been wrapped around his body like a tiny human blanket.

He found her staring at the patio doorway. "You're not going to believe this," Zoe said. "He's back."

"Who?" He yawned and reached across the covers to scratch a dozing Reynaldo's head.

"The swallow. I swear this house is part of his migration pattern. I opened the door to look outside and in he swooped. Look! There he is!" Arm extended, she scrambled toward the sofa. "Did you see him?"

"Actually, no."

"Well then, pay attention. We have to shoo him out of here."

"I would if you weren't prancing around in nothing but my open work shirt." An idea came to him. "And how do you know it's a swallow? This time of evening, it could just as easily be a bat."

Zoe shrieked and dove back to their nest of blankets. Laughing, Jake pulled her close. "Don't you remember what I taught you? If you leave the creature alone, he'll fly to safety all on his own."

"Your advice won't do me any good if safety involves tangling in my hair."

"Don't worry, I'll protect you."

"My hero."

"You better believe it," he murmured, giving her neck a playful bite.

Life, he decided, was good. He still had his demons. He had flashbacks, and there were nights

when the terrors struck hard and he woke up screaming. But there were also long stretches where the
memories stayed buried and on the bad nights, he
had Zoe to hold him. He had Zoe to help with a lot
of things.

She'd decided to move to Naushatucket at the end
of last summer, when they both realized they didn't
want to spend winter apart. It was Zoe who insisted
they stay. She'd fallen in love with the island. And
Jake...

Jake had fallen in love with her. Looking back,
he'd probably loved her all along, but the day he offered to move in with her was the day he finally
admitted it. He hadn't stopped loving her since.

Yes, he thought, life was pretty good. Only one
thing would make it better. He sat up and reached
behind the kindling box.

Zoe was back to looking for her winged nemesis.
"You know," she pointed out, "not every problem
resolves itself. Sometimes a creature—or person—
needs a little push."

"You mean like me?" he teased.

She smiled. "You, my love, needed a shove."

"How about a plunge?" He held out a small velvet
box.

Instantly, Zoe's playfulness disappeared. Those
gorgeous blue eyes of hers went as wide as saucers,
and she sat up. "Are you sure?"

"Positive." To his surprise, his hands were shaking

as he opened it to reveal the diamond inside. "I told you once that I hoped to dream of the future again. Now I can't imagine a future without you in it. I love you, Zoe Hamilton. Will you marry me?"

She beamed, warming his insides like he once hadn't dreamed possible. "There's nothing I'd rather do."

Winged creature forgotten, she wrapped her arms around his neck and showed him exactly what their future would hold.

* * * * *

AUGUST 2011
HARDBACK TITLES

ROMANCE

Bride for Real	Lynne Graham
From Dirt to Diamonds	Julia James
The Thorn in His Side	Kim Lawrence
Fiancée for One Night	Trish Morey
The Untamed Argentinian	Susan Stephens
After the Greek Affair	Chantelle Shaw
The Highest Price to Pay	Maisey Yates
Under the Brazilian Sun	Catherine George
There's Something About a Rebel...	Anne Oliver
The Crown Affair	Lucy King
Australia's Maverick Millionaire	Margaret Way
Rescued by the Brooding Tycoon	Lucy Gordon
Not-So-Perfect Princess	Melissa McClone
The Heart of a Hero	Barbara Wallace
Swept Off Her Stilettos	Fiona Harper
Mr Right There All Along	Jackie Braun
The Tortured Rebel	Alison Roberts
Dating Dr Delicious	Laura Iding

HISTORICAL

Married to a Stranger	Louise Allen
A Dark and Brooding Gentleman	Margaret McPhee
Seducing Miss Lockwood	Helen Dickson
The Highlander's Return	Marguerite Kaye

MEDICAL™

The Doctor's Reason to Stay	Dianne Drake
Career Girl in the Country	Fiona Lowe
Wedding on the Baby Ward	Lucy Clark
Special Care Baby Miracle	Lucy Clark

AUGUST 2011
LARGE PRINT TITLES

ROMANCE

Jess's Promise	Lynne Graham
Not For Sale	Sandra Marton
After Their Vows	Michelle Reid
A Spanish Awakening	Kim Lawrence
In the Australian Billionaire's Arms	Margaret Way
Abby and the Bachelor Cop	Marion Lennox
Misty and the Single Dad	Marion Lennox
Daycare Mum to Wife	Jennie Adams

HISTORICAL

Miss in a Man's World	Anne Ashley
Captain Corcoran's Hoyden Bride	Annie Burrows
His Counterfeit Condesa	Joanna Fulford
Rebellious Rake, Innocent Governess	Elizabeth Beacon

MEDICAL™

Cedar Bluff's Most Eligible Bachelor	Laura Iding
Doctor: Diamond in the Rough	Lucy Clark
Becoming Dr Bellini's Bride	Joanna Neil
Midwife, Mother...Italian's Wife	Fiona McArthur
St Piran's: Daredevil, Doctor...Dad!	Anne Fraser
Single Dad's Triple Trouble	Fiona Lowe

SEPTEMBER 2011
HARDBACK TITLES

ROMANCE

The Kanellis Scandal	Michelle Reid
Monarch of the Sands	Sharon Kendrick
One Night in the Orient	Robyn Donald
His Poor Little Rich Girl	Melanie Milburne
The Sultan's Choice	Abby Green
The Return of the Stranger	Kate Walker
Girl in the Bedouin Tent	Annie West
Once Touched, Never Forgotten	Natasha Tate
Nice Girls Finish Last	Natalie Anderson
The Italian Next Door...	Anna Cleary
From Daredevil to Devoted Daddy	Barbara McMahon
Little Cowgirl Needs a Mum	Patricia Thayer
To Wed a Rancher	Myrna Mackenzie
Once Upon a Time in Tarrula	Jennie Adams
The Secret Princess	Jessica Hart
Blind Date Rivals	Nina Harrington
Cort Mason – Dr Delectable	Carol Marinelli
Survival Guide to Dating Your Boss	Fiona McArthur

HISTORICAL

The Lady Gambles	Carole Mortimer
Lady Rosabella's Ruse	Ann Lethbridge
The Viscount's Scandalous Return	Anne Ashley
The Viking's Touch	Joanna Fulford

MEDICAL ROMANCE™

Return of the Maverick	Sue MacKay
It Started with a Pregnancy	Scarlet Wilson
Italian Doctor, No Strings Attached	Kate Hardy
Miracle Times Two	Josie Metcalfe

0811 Gen Std LP

SEPTEMBER 2011
LARGE PRINT TITLES

ROMANCE

Too Proud to be Bought	Sharon Kendrick
A Dark Sicilian Secret	Jane Porter
Prince of Scandal	Annie West
The Beautiful Widow	Helen Brooks
Rancher's Twins: Mum Needed	Barbara Hannay
The Baby Project	Susan Meier
Second Chance Baby	Susan Meier
Her Moment in the Spotlight	Nina Harrington

HISTORICAL

More Than a Mistress	Ann Lethbridge
The Return of Lord Conistone	Lucy Ashford
Sir Ashley's Mettlesome Match	Mary Nichols
The Conqueror's Lady	Terri Brisbin

MEDICAL ROMANCE™

Summer Seaside Wedding	Abigail Gordon
Reunited: A Miracle Marriage	Judy Campbell
The Man with the Locked Away Heart	Melanie Milburne
Socialite...or Nurse in a Million?	Molly Evans
St Piran's: The Brooding Heart Surgeon	Alison Roberts
Playboy Doctor to Doting Dad	Sue MacKay

Discover Pure Reading Pleasure with

Visit the Mills & Boon website for all the latest in romance

- **Buy** all the latest releases, backlist and eBooks

- **Join** our community and chat to authors and other readers

- **Win** with our fantastic online competitions

- **Tell us** what you think by signing up to our reader panel

- **Find out** more about our authors and their books

- **Free** online reads from your favourite authors

- **Sign** up for our free monthly eNewsletter

- **Rate** and review books with our star system

www.millsandboon.co.uk

 Follow us at twitter.com/millsandboonuk

 Become a fan at facebook.com/romancehq